Sadie reported, "Robin, did you hear? Sheriff Houtman found a body in the alley behind The Joker's Den this morning. According to the victim's tee shirt, he has a connection to the Lovey Doves' Bluegrass Band. No one knows who he is or how he ended up behind Tyler's Joker's Den. The sheriff roped off the alley and won't give anyone any details of what happened. I'm going back over there now to see if I can find out about anything else they've found, but I wanted you to know before someone burst into your store with the news. How can something like this happen in a safe town like Pittman? I didn't escape the atrocious ISIS murderers to be faced with the murder of another innocent young man." With that statement, Sadie ended the phone call.

I was dumbfounded. "A murder in our sleepy town?" I took my cold tea to the sink in the back of my bookstore and dumped the contents, hoping to dump the scary thoughts niggling at my imagination.

Ten minutes later, Sadie called again. She reported, "Deputy Murphy says they are starting a canvas of the neighborhood to see if anyone has seen any strangers in town. Meanwhile, Sheriff Houtman is interviewing Tyler at his Joker's Den to see what he knows about the victim. Tyler gets some suspicious-looking characters in his store."

Praise for Mary Ann Jacobs

One of my critics, Karen Martin, the author of the *Rabbit Hash Mystery Series*, commented that *Don't Mess with Me* is a delightful puzzle for the readers to solve.

Don't Mess with Me

by

Mary Ann Jacobs

The Berkshires Mystery Series

Don't Mess with Me

Cover Art by *Jennifer Greeff*

The Wild Rose Press, Inc.
PO Box 708
Adams Basin, NY 14410-0708
Visit us at www.thewildrosepress.com

Publishing History
First Edition, 2023
Trade Paperback ISBN978-1-5092-4764-6
Digital ISBN978-1-5092-4765-3

The Berkshires Mystery Series
Published in the United States of America

Dedication

I would like to thank the members of my Writers'
Workshop and all of my first readers who did a great
job of picking apart my manuscript and encouraging me
to continue writing.

Acknowledgments

I would like to thank my editors: Dottie Caster, Paula Wolfe, Elizabeth Coldren, Linda Mauser, and Karen Martin. I also appreciate my Geezers' Writing Group for listening to each chapter and making suggestions. I thank the many members of the Northern Kentucky Bridge Club for appreciating my poetry and insisting that I keep sending out a poem a day during the pandemic. Their encouragement kept me writing.

Chapter 1

Crash Landing

While sipping a steaming cup of green tea from my favorite mug, I was daydreaming about the times when Asher and his dad skied those slopes at Jiminy Creek and the Bousquet Ski areas. Asher was so proud of himself when he graduated from the bunny slope. "I did it, Mom. I skied all the way down the big people's slope." I laughed just thinking of the excited and proud look on his eleven-year-old face.

My thoughts turned to his proud dad, and I yearned for John's company. I still found myself looking for him to enter the room and come over to hug me or ruffle Asher's blonde hair. It's been over three years since we lost him.

I jumped when the phone rang and interrupted my memories. I went to pick it up.

"Robin, did you hear? Sheriff Houtman found a body in the alley behind The Joker's Den this morning. According to the victim's T-shirt, he has a connection to the Lovey Doves' Bluegrass Band. No one knows who he is or how he ended up behind Tyler's Joker's Den. The sheriff roped off the alley and won't give anyone any details of what happened. I'm going back over there now to see if I can find out about anything else they've found, but I wanted you to know before someone burst into your store with the news. How can something like this happen in a safe town like Pittman? I didn't escape the atrocious ISIS murderers to be faced with the murder of another innocent young man." With that statement, Sadie ended the phone call.

I was dumbfounded. "*A murder in our sleepy town?*" I took my cold tea to the sink in the back of my bookstore and emptied the contents, hoping to dump the scary thoughts niggling at my imagination.

Ten minutes later, Sadie called again. She reported, "Deputy Murphy says they are starting a canvas of the neighborhood to see if anyone has seen any strangers in town. Meanwhile, Sheriff Houtman is interviewing Tyler at his Joker's Den to see what he knows about the victim. Tyler gets some suspicious-looking characters in his store. Who knows what kind of business transactions take place in the backroom? I keep a wary lookout at his customers in case any of the ISIS hitmen from our village come looking for me. I wasn't exactly popular with the fighters who took over our village. If they ever sneak over the border here looking for people from the Lebanese underground fighters, I'm sure I will be at the top of their hit list, and The Joker's Den would be the type of place they would seek out.

Sadie continued, "I'll be over to the bookstore as soon as I take care of our remaining customers. Most of my usual afternoon customers are out on the street watching the murder scene and hoping to get some information."

I put down the phone, trying to make sense of what Sadie said. Just then, my front door chime clanged loudly. I jerked around and saw a dripping wet blob crash into my bookshop. Not a sight I wanted to see with a murderer on the prowl.

"Bummer cold out there," said the tall teenaged boy as he shook off the snowflakes from his jacket sleeves. He was dressed in a torn T-shirt and jeans with more than fashionable holes in them. For a coat, he wore a tattered denim jacket that he had outgrown. His black hair was long, messy, and hadn't met with a pair of scissors in a while. He reminded me of the scarecrow in the *Wizard of Oz*. His smile, though, was quite infectious, so much so that I couldn't keep from smiling back at him. He certainly didn't look like a murderer.

"Got anything to warm a kid up, like hot chocolate or coffee with lots of cream?" Then this smiling stranger stuck out his hand and said, "Hey, I'm Billy. Who are you?"

"Well, hey to you, Billy. I'm Robin George, the owner of this bookstore where you practically broke down the door."

"Sorry about that. Clumsy me tripped over the step by the door. I trip a lot." Billy laughed. "My feet are just too big, and my long legs often put me off balance. You should see me try to ski. It's like rubber man slipping and sliding down the hills, fall, snap back up, fall, snap back up. At least I'm able to get back up."

I appraised this door crasher. I hadn't seen this kid before. His appearance intrigued me. Billy looked to be about fourteen or fifteen, but it was hard to tell because of his demeanor and carefree manner. I liked his jaunty attitude and friendliness. Billy didn't look like the visiting tourists who came to Pittman in anticipation of an early start to the ski season, and he didn't fit a murderer's profile.

"I'd like to see rubber man on the slopes. You must

create quite the scene. You should wear a sign on your back, 'Beware the Meandering Rubber Man.' Do you ski here often, or are you new to our area, Billy?" I waited for an answer, but he ignored me. I stared at him as he started doing jumping jacks to warm up. He looked like those dolls whose arms and legs you can pull into all shapes.

Billy then heard the giggles from the story corner, stopped jumping, and ran over to see what was going on. On his way, awkward Billy managed to bump into the shelf with all the stuffed animals, knocking a rubber ducky and Curious George to the floor. He flashed me an embarrassed grin, and said, "Sorry, Ms. George, I told you I'm clumsy." He then headed straight to the Story Corner.

Chapter 2

Billy's Strange Reaction to the Dragon Book

I followed Billy warily. I loved our Story Corner with its stage and pew-like benches filled with eager preschoolers, and I didn't want the parents to be wary of this scruffy door crasher. They might feel that he's a threat to their children.

Lola, our wanna-be actress turned storyteller, was just beginning to act out a children's book. I regarded her with a motherly fondness. If John and I had been blessed with a daughter, I imagined that she would be similar to Lola. I looked back at Lola's red hair flying all over as she smiled at the small children who eagerly awaited her story. She then began her humorous portrayal of a bumbling dragon. "Once upon a time in Loopy Land, far away lived a hiccupping dragon named Fire. His cave was deep in the snowy mountains."

Billy was staring at Lola and listening with an amazed look on his face.

Lola hid behind the lumpy green sofa in our Story Corner, but she was so tall that the kids could see her head peeking out at them. As the little ones giggled, Lola continued. "Fire was afraid to come out in the winter because each time he opened his mouth to speak, he would hiccup loudly, and that caused arrows of fire to shoot out of his huge mouth. This wasn't too bad in the summer because Fire could stomp out the sparks with his big feet, but in the winter, before he could stomp the fire out, his flames caused the snow to melt and start down the mountain in mini avalanches. These avalanches were a danger during ski season. Warnings were posted at all the ski lodges, 'Danger! Watch out for falling snow and rocks!'

"Hiccup, Hiccup—Oh no. Here I go again." Peals of laughter erupted as Lola stumbled around the room hiccupping.

"Look out, Fire," yelled the children. Billy stood staring at Lola. When the children laughed, Billy just stared. When the kids looked on in awe, Billy stared. When they began to clap and chant, "Fire, Fire," Billy continued to stare. Billy ignored everyone except Lola.

When the children and parents left, the children continued the hiccupping routine. While Lola and I ushered the families out, Billy stayed behind and grabbed the dragon book from the table and frantically flipped through the pages. "Fire, is that really you? I can't believe it. I've missed you so." Billy patted the large red dragon on the cover. Waving the book over his head, Billy jumped up high and yelled, "Whoop, whoop, whoopee!" Then Billy fell to the carpeted floor, put his head on the book, and began to sob.

I rushed back into the Story Corner spotting him sitting, holding the book, and crying. What was wrong with this strange boy? I started toward him, not sure what to do. "Billy, what's the matter? Why are you sobbing so? Can I help you with something? Did you hurt yourself?"

I handed him some tissues. Through his sobs, Billy choked out, "Fire is really here. I thought she made him up. I thought Aunt Dehlia was crazy, but here he is. You found him. Thank you, Ms. George, thank you."

"Who is Aunt Dehlia, and why would she make up a story about a hiccupping dragon?" I asked the desperate boy.

Billy didn't answer. Exhausted from crying, he fell in a heap and curled up in the corner, hugging the book, *Fire, the Hiccupping Dragon* as if it were a long-lost treasure. With hair askew and reddened eyes, Billy sniffled and again patted the picture of the dragon. His arrogance disappeared, and he looked just like the forlorn Oliver in Dickens' novel.

I went over to the corner and patted him on the back to comfort him, but Billy turned away, embarrassed. He covered his head with his arms, but he still held on tightly to the dragon book. I decided to give him space. I walked over to the bookshelves and began to straighten up the story corner waiting for Sadie to arrive with more news. When I next looked at Billy, the young man was sound asleep on my beige rug, snoring like a hibernating bear, still hugging *Fire, the Hiccupping Dragon.*

I went over and nudged Billy to wake him, but, as only exhausted teenage boys can do, he wasn't about to wake up from his deep sleep. I squeezed his hands and even tickled his arm. No response. *"You're just like my son. Asher could sleep through an earthquake or hurricane."* Feeling motherly, I took the plaid throw from the couch and covered him gently, but I was worried.

As I looked out the large picture window of my Bookworm Shop on Farley Square, snow was floating down from the gray sky. Pittman was beginning to resemble a proper ski resort town. Maybe this mysterious stranger will add intrigue to the Berkshire ski season.

"Even though the Sheriff and Deputy are busy trying to solve a gruesome murder, at least the skiers will be excited about an early opening to the season."

We have two major ski venues nearby, and though it is only the beginning of November, the snow-making machines have been cranked up, and people will flock here soon to conquer the slopes. Families bring their children for lessons with our experienced skiing instructor, who often has the kids graduating from the beginner hill to the larger slopes by the age of five or six. Pros enjoy the many expert slopes in the beautiful mountains. Race teams of all ages practice and compete throughout the season. In a good year, tourists begin their invasion in November and keep coming through the winter months.

I wonder if Billy came with his family for a ski vacation. I looked over at the sleeping bear and felt protective of him though I wasn't sure why.

Chapter 3

Where Is Sadie?

"Why isn't Sadie here yet?" I spouted.

Sadie is my best friend in Pittman, and her phone call troubled me. Murders never happened in this small tight-knit community. Could this stranger in my store be responsible for the murder in the alley? But if Billy's guilty, why would he crash into my bookstore and introduce himself? Maybe he's looking for a hiding place to escape detection. If he is a murderer, you'd think he'd head out of Pittman as fast as possible, putting miles of mountains between himself and the murder victim instead of curling up and falling asleep.

Perhaps he doesn't have transportation. He's too young to drive; bus service is practically nonexistent in our town, and he doesn't look like he has money to hire a ride-share company or taxi. I don't think I'm in the presence of a murderer, but you never can tell.

Mysterious Billy isn't our typical book buyer, either. He looks destitute, and I wonder if he reads books at all. Why is he here and so excited about a children's book? Where does he live, and who is this Aunt Dehlia?

As questions popped into my head, I knew I should call the sheriff right away in case Billy is connected to the surprising murder. The timing of his appearance is certainly suspicious. Perhaps the sheriff can track down Billy's parents and figure out who he is. But, instead of calling Mark Houtman, I run to my Mickey Mouse phone and again call Sadie. I left a frantic message, "Sadie, get over here now. Where are you? I might be in my store with a murderer."

Sadie had used her wits to escape ISIS in Lebanon. Problem-solving Sadie will know what to do about this possible suspect. I'm sure she'll have a better plan than our bumbling sheriff who tends to act first then think later.

Minutes later, Sadie, black hair all windblown and still wearing her flour-stained baking apron over her black pant suit, burst into my shop, and shouted, "What do you mean a possible murderer might be in your store?" Following my pointing, Sadie walked over to the prone figure on the floor in the Storytelling Corner.

"This young man, who appeared out of nowhere, is Billy, and he just fell asleep after acting crazy while spouting something about a missing dragon. Sadie, I don't know what to do. He's sound asleep, and I can't seem to wake him. Do you think he's okay? He seems harmless, but what do you think? Should I call Sheriff Houtman?" I blurted out.

Shaking her head, my unflappable friend said, "The sheriff's a little busy right now. Hold off while we get a grip on who this kid is. I just left the crime scene and went back to Sweet Indulgences to reassure my customers. I had just locked up and was heading over here when you called. Mark and Deputy Murphy are perplexed. No one recognizes the victim. Sheriff Houtman has the crime photographer from the local paper taking pictures. I heard Deputy Murphy tell Mark that the victim didn't have a wallet or ID, so it could be a robbery gone wrong."

Sadie continued, "I know Sheriff Houtman investigated murders when he worked in Boston, but our small town is a more comfortable and safer environment in contrast to the big city. Though I've wondered more than once why Sheriff Houtman opted for small-town life, I'm sure the simple life of Pittman was one thing that drew him here. Let's hope his investigative work in Boston translates to finding a local murderer. The sheriff doesn't always inspire confidence since he's so arrogant and seldom listens to the locals."

As she spoke, Sadie looked at Billy and lowered her agile five-foot-two frame down next to our mysterious stranger and started to search Billy's tattered pants' pockets. Empty.

"What are you doing? Robbing him isn't a good idea."

"I'm not robbing him, Stupida. I am looking for some identification to figure out who he is so we can locate his parents." Sadie took his worn jacket that had fallen next to him and emptied the pockets. She only found one candy bar, a pack of matches, and a rumpled business card from the Berkshire Bank with the name Dehlia scrawled on the back.

I interrupted her investigation. "Dehlia, that's the name Billy kept saying over and over. She has something to do with this hiccupping dragon in the book Lola was reading."

As Sadie continued searching Billy, she found no identification and no money in his wallet.

"Look at this, Robin."

Around his neck, Billy had a dirty shoelace chain that had a locket dangling from it, and a gold charm in the shape of a dragon. Sadie, being careful not to break her newly manicured nails or to wake Billy, opened the rusted silver locket and found a lock of hair and a faded picture of a woman of about twenty years of age dressed in jeans and a plaid untucked shirt, and wearing flip-flops. "I wonder who this woman is?" Sadie murmured. On the floor beside Billy's jacket, Sadie saw something shiny. She stooped to pick up a key that looked like a safe deposit key.

"Why would a teenage boy carry around a safe deposit key?" I asked. Billy was still a mystery.

"Okay, Robin," Sadie said, "you know, we must call Houtman and get him to check Billy's background, no matter how mad he'll be with us, or how busy he is. He'll only get angrier if we wait to tell him about Billy. A scruffy stranger appearing at about the same time as a murder is suspicious, and I don't want to experience the wrath of Houtman again because we withheld evidence, even though I'm sure he'll dismiss any evidence we present. Cute as Sheriff Mark Houtman is, he sure has a temper."

Sadie was right. Her instincts were always spot on. I need to listen to her advice more often, especially when Sheriff Houtman is involved. Sadie Aboud has a remarkable ability to read people. She's been my best friend since I moved to Pittman from Kentucky and is an immigrant who escaped from Lebanon via a relief organization. She developed a sense of wariness as she avoided ISIS thugs who were trying to find the insurgents in the underground of which Sadie was a member. Her ability to anticipate people's reactions saved her life many times.

Sadie told me her sad tale the first time we had coffee together at Sweet Indulgences. She said her parents were rousted from their home in Beirut, dragged into the street, and shot by a gang of ISIS fighters. Sadie and her ten-year-old brother fled out the back door of their house, hiding until the fighters left, continuing their rampage through Sadie's small village. Both children then began a frightening adventure until they found safety in the refugee camp.

After living in appalling conditions in the camp for close to a year, Sadie's visa was approved. Since she had an aunt in Pittman with a successful restaurant, Sadie was granted refugee status and came to live with her Aunt Florence. Her aunt was so pleased to have family around that she gave her dejected and scared niece a job in the bakery/restaurant, Sweet Indulgences, which is two doors down from my bookstore. I can smell the tempting aromas each day as I open my shop.

The tourists love the gooey baked goods and wonderful Lebanese food served at Sweet Indulgences. Sadie became a hit, ready to make any newcomer or visitor feel at home. The teenagers love it when Sadie does a comedic routine about a little boy eating his first chocolate ice cream cone. By the last "Drip, drip, oh no," the teens are laughing aloud.

Sadie is every customer's friend. Because Aunt Florence is getting up in age, Sadie now does all the heavy lifting, stocking, ordering, and menu planning. Throughout the year, locals go to Sweet Indulgences, not just for the melt-in-your-mouth pastries, but also for Sadie's humor. As a now confident person, it amazes me that someone who arrived so scared and sad has emerged with a great sense of humor. My customers have confided in me that when they feel depressed or isolated, they head over to the café just to laugh with Sadie. I told Sadie that she should convert part of the restaurant into a comedy club during the summer for a few nights a week. That would certainly be a draw for the theater lovers that flock to the Berkshires.

Since she arrived in Pittman, Sadie has been not only my friend but my confidant and partner in crime. Unfortunately, over the past three years, we have stumbled upon some bizarre happenings that made Sheriff Mark Houtman certain that we were partners in troublemaking. This situation with Billy will further solidify the sheriff's image of us as meddlers. If Billy has anything to do with the robbery or murder, I know Sheriff Houtman will not want us meddling in a murder investigation. Only his admiration of Sadie will save us from his lecture. I went to the phone and hesitatingly placed a call to the sheriff.

"He's busy right now," said his clerk. "There's been a murder, and Sheriff Houtman and Deputy Murphy are at the scene. I'll have him call you as soon as he returns."

"Maggie, it's really important," I said. "Sadie and I might have information about the murderer. Please get the message to him right away."

Chapter 4

Memories: The Bookworm Shop's Beginning

After Sadie's examination of the still sleeping Billy, she went back to Sweet Indulgences. It was quiet in my Bookworm Shop. The parents and children from Story Hour had gone, and Lola was taking a well-deserved break. I relished the quiet so I would have time to think. As I was waiting for the Sheriff to return my call, I began to reminisce.

I started The Bookworm Shop after the fatal heart attack of my husband John, who was, I thought, a healthy fifty-year-old. My kind and intelligent husband collapsed on the soccer field where he was coaching my son Asher's team. The ambulance was on site, so they rushed him to the hospital, but it was too late. At the funeral, other parents would say, "Well, at least you know that he didn't suffer."

Their words were no comfort. I was devastated, angry, abandoned, and a now single mother of an inconsolable eleven-year-old son who loved his dad so much. I didn't know how to comfort Asher when I felt so horribly sad. How could I tell him that everything would be okay when I didn't believe that?

John and I had planned to do so many things together. We had tickets to go to Germany and visit as many castles as possible throughout Europe. John was going to take Asher to the soccer stadiums and even had booked tickets to one of the games.

"Please, John, please," I had begged, "my number one adventure is to go to the Grand Canyon during Spring Break. I have always pictured you, Asher, and me astride donkeys descending the narrow path to the Canyon floor. I went there once with my grandfather when I was ten, and I always have wanted to return."

When we retired after Asher went off to college, we were going to buy a cottage in one of our favorite spots by the sea near Cape Cod. Evenings we would dream of cruises to the Caribbean, Italy, and even a Mediterranean cruise. We were ready for so many adventures.

No Germany, no soccer games, no cottage by the sea, no cruises, no Grand Canyon, no John, my beloved husband, the father of my now fatherless son. Now all those dreams were like yesterday's sunshine, gone. Left in its place was this gray cloud encompassing my heart.

At John's funeral, Asher turned to me and said, "Mom, Dad had an excellent job. Now that he is gone, will we be poor? Will we be homeless and forced to eat from dumpsters? You know, I get hungry, especially after junior high marching band practice. Do you want me to get a job? I think Mr. Green will hire me to clean up his meat market. I won't make much because I'm only eleven, but maybe the money I earn will be enough to buy food."

I looked at him through my tears, so like his father, with dark hair, large expressive eyes that mirrored his soul, five feet tall already with that determined jawline, willing to lend a hand to all. I loved that he was ready to step up and take his father's place as breadwinner.

My heart broke just a little bit more. I took a deep breath and said, "No, Asher, you don't have to go to work. You just concentrate on being the great student that your dad always wanted you to be.

Your mom has a plan. You will have plenty to eat, I assure you." Then I rubbed his hair, rolled my eyes, and thought, *"Robin, girl, you better get a plan, and soon, or this promise is down the drain."*

A year after John's death, I decided to leave my home in Kentucky that I loved. Without John, I had a tough time socializing with our friends who were wonderful to me, but who were couples, and I felt the memories of us all getting together as couples to share our lives was something to cherish, but I knew I needed to move on with my life.

I needed a change of scenery, a new beginning. After talking it over with my closest friend, Paula, I decided to get a fresh start. My life as a single parent needed new horizons. We discussed how many of our friends have relocated to Massachusetts in various towns in the Berkshires for winter skiing and year-round theater.

John, Asher, and I spent relaxing vacations in the Berkshires skiing the mountain slopes from beginner to expert. In the summer we attended the summer festivals. I started laughing as I described to Paula a summer Bluegrass festival in Pittman. As we sat on our blankets listening to the great music, I looked up. I saw a long line of cows going for milking. "Look, John," I said, "they can barely carry their bodies forward because their udders are so filled with milk. I've never seen such a sight." That was the same day that Asher saw baby pigs being born in the barn at the festival.

John, having grown up on a farm in Kentucky, of course, just made fun of my city girl expressions when I witnessed these country happenings.

Paula and I poured over real estate listings in Pittman, Lennon, and Stockbridge. I found a quaint little house in Pittman on the same street where we had rented a condo one summer. "Paula, it's perfect. It's right off the main street and is walking distance to Asher's middle school and eventually his high school." Paula was such a help to me as I worked out all the complicated details of buying property and moving from safe, familiar Kentucky to the East. I promised that we would stay connected through video chats. We both marked our calendars right then with a date for Paula and her family to visit us that summer.

When Asher and I settled in our new home, Asher signed up for a theater camp for four weeks and a soccer camp for two weeks. He figured that was the best way to make friends during the summer before he started band camp two weeks before school started.

Meanwhile, I developed a plan to start my own business. I had always dreamed of owning a bookstore. My love of books was insatiable. When I heard that Mr. Alexander was selling his Dry Cleaners on Farley Square in Pittman, I decided to take the leap and made an offer. Pittman was about three hours from Cape Cod, where John and I had dreamed of moving after we retired. I'm not retired, but this small town needs a bookstore. None of Mr. Alexander's children were interested in the family dry cleaning business, so he was willing to sell the rundown building for a fair price. He remembered Asher and me from our trips when Asher was little. Mr. Alexander always had a cup of warm hot chocolate ready for all those who dropped off their dry cleaning.

Thus, I wound up owning this property in the heart of Farley Square. Transforming a dry-cleaning business into a bookstore was a challenge, but I needed a challenge and a job. The store now sports a green canopy on which sits a wooden sign painted by Asher. It depicts a giant smiling bookworm with red plaid glasses next to a pile of scattered books. Remodeling took me almost three months of calling in all my friends and Asher's new friends from his camps to build bookshelves, sew curtains, and paint each room with cheerful colors. The artistic teenagers decorated the Story Corner in the Children's section with drawings of cute animals holding books. The Mystery section sported a funny caricature of Sherlock Holmes, cap, pipe, and all. The Science Fiction section was devoted to pictures from Star Wars movies and Star Trek TV shows.

With all this wonderful emotional support from friends and family, I was determined to open in November in time for holiday buying. The Farley Square merchants encouraged me to join in the holiday promotions and festivities they set up for the town of Pittman. I was so grateful for their acceptance and encouragement, so I charged right into the neighborhood merchants' festivities and never regretted it. Those merchants became my friends and support group.

Though small bookstores are a dying breed, we at the Bookworm Shop pride ourselves on our unique selection of children's books and try to give individual attention to each customer. Stacks of colorful picture books fill a brilliant yellow corner of the store. Groupings of paperbacks line the bookshelves arranged by interest levels, from beginning readers to thick fantasy novels. Nowhere in all the surrounding small towns in the Berkshires, can customers find a more extensive range of children's books.

My customers consider the Bookworm Shop a meeting place for those interested in literature for themselves, their children, and grandchildren. Story Time for Preschoolers is one of the families' favorite programs.

After three years of building my business, I know most of the people in and around Pittman and entice them into my shop with mystery nights, dramas, guest authors, and story times. One of our most successful programs is a night of books and poetry. Now fifteen, Asher and his fellow band members are regulars and often read the funniest poems they have written or found, making the audience break out with laughter. During the summer months of the play festivals, many screenwriters and actors come into the shop and end up as guest speakers at our literary guest night, where we serve appetizers to a sizeable group of tourists and residents.

Life in the summer is great, and business is brisk because of the numerous book-loving tourists. Since visitors from Boston, New York, and far-flung areas of the country flock here for the summer stock theater season, we do a huge business with our inventory of plays and books on stagecraft. A visiting actor or director often signs books and posters, which always boosts sales. We also have an extensive collection of all things Shakespeare since Shakespeare and Company in

Stockbridge is a great tourist destination. Sporting three stages, this venue brings to the Berkshires devoted fans of the Bard.

During the winter, I need to count on the locals and the skiers to keep my venture going. Lola is a great help to me in the store. She not only serves as my entertainer but also, she is my best employee and keeps the store going with her flair for bookkeeping and promotions to keep the store afloat.

Interrupting my trip down memory lane, two teenage boys burst into the store, laughing hysterically. I said, "Now what are you two up to?"

Chapter 5

Revelations

"Did you see Ms. Marshall's face yesterday when she saw all the blood? I must give her credit. She didn't panic but very calmly sent the girl seated next to the door to get another teacher and then the principal," laughed Asher.

"What is so funny about blood, you hooligans?" I said to my son, Asher, and his best friend, Mike, who were dripping melting snow all over my rug. They couldn't stop laughing. Finally, Mike choked out, "Freddy hit Jose with a stapler, and then Jose had to get staples in his forehead to stop the bleeding. Now I know what irony means. Freddie's dad grounded him, so he won't be at the band competition this evening."

I just frowned at them. "Don't sweat the small things," Sadie often told me.

Lola returned from her coffee break so the boys quickly changed the subject.

Asher asked Lola and me, "Did you hear the terrible news? Klette's Pharmacy was robbed last night. They stole hundreds of dollars and bottles of Oxy Contin and other pain pills. He's owned that pharmacy for over ten years, and nothing like that has ever happened. Mr. Klette is such a great guy. His son Dan plays the drums in the marching band with us. Mr.

Klette and his wife come to every competition. Every Wednesday night practice, Mrs. Klette brings the best chocolate chip cookies that melt in your mouth. Mr. Klette is one of the parents who loads and unloads our instruments for every competition. Both are respected by all the band members."

"Who would do something so awful to such nice people?" Lola asked. "They devote their lives to that store and care about every customer. When my friend Jana had cancer and couldn't afford some of her medicine, Mr. Klette put out a donation jar to collect money to pay for the pills. He accepted the payment of whatever was collected and never charged her another penny.

"But the worst thing that's happened," Mike added, "is that this morning some man was found dead in the alley across the street from the pharmacy behind The Joker's Den. There was blood all over. The sheriff is trying to identify him now. He was dressed in scrubby jeans and a black T-shirt with LOVEY DOVES' BLUEGRASS BAND on the front. Benny, the tuba player in our band, was taking a shortcut through the alley on his way to school when he found the victim, and wow, was Benny freaked out. He started yelling and ran into the street, stopping all the cars while screaming, 'Murder, murder, help, help.'"

"We were also on our way to school and ran to see what all the commotion was," Asher said. "We saw the twisted body, and it was evident from all the blood that it wasn't an accident. The sheriff arrived and made us leave because it was a crime scene, but not before we heard him send for the coroner and confirm to Deputy Murphy that it looked like a murder."

"Did Sadie tell you any more about the victim's death?" asked Mike. "We saw her talking to Sheriff Houtman."

"No, just that he didn't have a wallet or ID."

Asher interrupted. "The Joker's Den was also trashed last night. Broken furniture and goods were scattered all over. Of course, Mopey Tyler, the owner, says he doesn't think anything was taken from The Joker's Den, but that's probably because he doesn't want anyone to know he sells racy merchandise in his back room, and he wasn't about to produce an inventory of his store's contents. Many people say they don't think it's flour in those bins in the front of his store, but that it's heroin or some other drug."

"Did you say the man's T-shirt had Lovey Doves' Bluegrass Band on it?" Lola asked, looking like she had seen a ghost.

"Lola, do you know anything about this man?" I asked.

"I...I may have heard my mom talk about a Bluegrass band called the Lovey Doves. I think her boyfriend might have had some connection to it."

We all stared at Lola. Could she know the murder victim? Just then, the phone rang. It was Sadie. She started to tell me about the break-ins so I told her to come over to hear what Mike and Asher just told us.

When Sadie arrived, she asked, "What's going on? What do the boys know?"

Lola quickly deflected my question aimed at her connection to the band. Lola said, "I think Tyler might have trashed The Joker's Den to throw suspicion off himself. Maybe Tyler stole the money and drugs from the pharmacy so he could resell the drugs in his shady business dealings. I've seen some strange customers enter his shop through the alley."

"The murdered man," Sadie started, "might be a partner of Tyler's or hired to steal the drugs so Tyler could resell them to his 'clients.' Tyler's someone who deserves some bad luck. He is so grouchy and hates anyone unless they're buyers for his smut and drugs. I sure know he hates me. You should hear the names he shouts at me. I think all the merchants on Farley Square would agree that Tyler is evil enough to commit murder."

I was about to confront Lola about her connection to the victim when Asher continued, "When Sheriff Houtman showed up, we had Benny sitting on the curb while we tried to calm him down. Deputy Murphy knew Benny from soccer, so the Deputy took over and finally got Benny to lead them to the victim."

Sadie and I went into detective mode and started to throw out more questions at the boys. Sadie said, "Sheriff Houtman wouldn't let me get close enough to the crime scene to get a good look at the victim."

I asked, "Did either of you get a good look at the victim? Do you think he's from around here?"

"We've told you all we know about the break-ins and the murder victim in the alley. The sheriff kept us from getting close enough to see the guy's face, but Benny remembered the writing on the T-shirt. The sheriff's trying to keep everything quiet, so he made us leave when Deputy Murphy went into the alley," Mike said.

"Lola, maybe the sheriff has a picture of the victim so you can see if you recognize him as a member of your mom's band, or could he be your mom's boyfriend from the band?"

At first, Lola didn't answer. I looked at her. She looked away and said, "I don't see how it could be my mom's boyfriend or any of her band members. The band disbanded after my mom's death." Lola quickly turned and headed to the back of the shop, giving no further details.

Sadie looked at me in astonishment. "Did you know that Lola's mom is dead?"

"First, I've heard of it. I just thought she didn't have a good relationship with her mother. Lola seemed so friendly with Jana that I thought Jana might be a friend of her mother's. Lola certainly left us in a hurry. Why do I get the feeling she's hiding something?"

Chapter 6

Identity Revealed

When the boys finished telling Sadie and me about the murder and vandalism, they spotted Billy snoring away on my rug.

"What is he doing here?" they both asked as they pointed at Billy.

"Do you know him?" Sadie and I both asked in surprise.

"Yeah," said Asher. "He's a new mysterious kid from our school."

Mike piped in. "Billy's a little weird, but can he ever draw, and what a mouth. He started playing the mellophone in our marching band. He blows so well; he sounds like a professional. When we asked him where he learned to play, he shrugged and said he just picked it up from his grandpa, who was a great musician, and from playing in a neighborhood band. We asked him where he had gone to school, but he quickly changed the subject. Since he came about two months ago, our band has won each competition. He's also playing the French horn in the orchestra."

"No one seems to know where Billy is from," Asher said, "or even where he now lives. He's secretive about anything personal. Some of his classmates say they've spotted him early in the morning showering in the school locker room. We think he could be homeless, or he just doesn't like to shower at home. I asked Billy why he went to the locker room each morning before class, and why his hair was always wet in the morning, and he answered, 'I like to have a wet head. It wakes me up, so I go to the gym and put my head in the shower each day. I have physics first period and can't think without my wet hair. It works better than having a cup of coffee.' I'm not sure I believe him. I never heard of a person needing to have wet hair to think. Obviously, Billy is lying. He's a strange one, but he seems like an okay guy."

I whispered to Sadie, "If there's an excuse that doesn't hold water, it's Billy's reason for a wet head, but the boys seem to accept Billy. We'll have to do some snooping at the school. If he's been here for two months, he's not such a stranger. Maybe he has no connection to the murder."

I knew the band was a tight group. If Asher and Mike respected Billy after only two months, then there must be more to this kid than meets the eye. I just hoped he didn't have any connection to the dead body in the alley. I have a funny feeling that Sheriff Houtman is going to look very suspiciously at anyone he doesn't know in town, particularly someone as scruffy as Billy, who seems to have appeared out of nowhere.

"We're going back to The Joker's Den to see if anyone knows any more about the murder," said Asher, and the boys rushed toward the door, waving at Sadie and me.

Before they stepped out the door, I stopped them. "This murder is horrible. Because nothing like this ever happens in this quiet town, I want you boys to stick close to home or the bookstore for the next few days. You're not to be wandering around town alone until the sheriff gets to the bottom of this and catches the killer and the vandals. A murderer is wandering about in our town, and I don't want you boys near any danger. Mike, that goes for you too, even if your dad doesn't say that."

Sadie agreed. "Mike and Asher, you can come to my shop also, but stay clear of Mike's dad's bowling alley. There are sometimes suspicious-looking characters at Ten Pins, particularly on Thursday evenings, and he is friendly with Tyler, who I wouldn't trust with anything. I'd bet anyone that he's involved in any crime that has happened."

After the boys left, Sadie looked at Billy snoring away on my rug, and said, "Poor kid. I wonder where he came from, and where he lives now? Do you think he could be homeless?" Sadie lost her only brother Joseph, who would be about Billy's age. It's taken a long time for her to rise above her depression over Joseph's loss and the circumstances in which he died. She has a soft spot now for all neglected kids. I can see that Billy's appearance has brought back these sad memories.

Sadie continued. "I watch out for Mike because his dad Sam is such a shady character. Do you all know Sam served time for a felony and then opened the Ten Pins, Bowling Alley when he was released from prison? I wonder where he got the money for the down payment. I'm sure Chester Fergusson would demand a hefty sum before selling to a felon. For the last couple of months, Ten Pins hasn't been doing well, according to the neighborhood gossip, and the merchants are curious about how Mike's dad is making ends meet. Mike avoids Sam as much as possible. I suspect Sam has been or is abusive to Mike. He's such a sweet kid. I really care about him."

Sadie loves it when the local teenagers stop into Sweet Indulgences for an after-school treat. Aunt Florence, now in her seventies, has dreams of retiring and touring the US with her friends. This year, Aunt Florence began treating Sadie as an equal partner and plans to have her take over Sweet Indulgences when she retires and embarks on her journeys.

Each day, teenagers fill the quaint shop with laughter as they sip their milkshakes and feast on the yummy small sandwiches on delicious pita bread that Sadie serves. Sadie hovers over them like a mother hen, the reason the teenagers see her as a caring soul and often turn to her in times of trouble.

Sadie is ready to help any kid with a problem. She is making a project of breaking down Mike's barriers and engaging him in a conversation that will reveal why he avoids his dad, but Mike is tight-lipped. Instead of sharing his personal stories, he tries to divert Sadie's attention by making jokes. Sadie thinks his humor is masking his pain.

"Robin, I am sure something terrible is going on in Mike's life. When the counselor at his high school came into the restaurant the other day, I told her my suspicions, but she said that Mike hasn't shared anything with her. I wish he would trust me enough to confide in me. I need to garner his trust. Mike has such a winning personality. His classmates, who frequent my shop, think he is great. When you see him with just Asher, you can tell that Asher respects Mike and that their bond goes deeper than just a casual friendship. Mike is hiding something that bothers him, and I think Asher knows his secret. I wish one of them would open up to me about what is going on."

Sadie turned to look at Billy, and tears filled her eyes. He reminded her of her brother Joseph, curled up on a rug before they fled their home in Lebanon, and then hiding out with her in the ruins of buildings bombed by ISIS. How scared they were, and Joseph was so young, only ten. Sadie wanted more than anything to protect him. How hungry they were when they were on the run, but they were determined to survive. Sadly, Joseph never made it out of Lebanon.

"I thought I had left all the killing ISIS fighters behind in Lebanon, but now we have a murder right here on Farley Square." Sadie shuddered as she relived the horrors from her past life. She had shared with me a little of what happened as she fled her home, but Sadie was still secretive about the hardships she faced before and after she arrived at the refugee camp in Lebanon. I never pushed her to reveal the tragedies, but she has told me about the terrifying nightmares she has. In time, I am confident she will open up to me.

Shaking off painful memories, Sadie said, "We must help Billy. If Sheriff Houtman sees Billy, a relative stranger, and a grungy one at that, the impetuous sheriff will think he was involved in the robbery, murder, or vandalism. Let's wake Billy up and question him so we can clear him before Sheriff Houtman comes poking around. If Billy is as smart as the boys think he is, he'll see that we care about him, and he has a chance to earn our trust. I'll explain to him that if he gives us some honest answers, then we can protect him from the sheriff's inept questioning."

After we flung all our questions at Asher and Mike and issued our orders, I went back to the Story Corner, where Lola was tidying up, stacking the kid-sized benches, and putting away the folding chairs.

I try not to question Lola much about her past life, but sometimes I wonder if I should have probed a bit further. She is a secretive person. At twenty-five, she is vivacious, tall, and beautiful and has a wonderfully expressive face. When Lola arrived in Pittman, she told me she left her home in Chicago to try her hand at Hollywood, landing a few commercial gigs, but soon ended up jobless with no money to pay the high apartment rental fees in LA. I asked her why she came to Pittman rather than going to her mom's house in Chicago. I didn't want to pry, but I felt sorry for her. She seemed so vulnerable behind her happy demeanor.

Lola said, "My best friend and mentor, Jana, who works in the costume department at Shakespeare and Company in Stockbridge, was extremely ill. That's why I returned to the Berkshires rather than deal with defeat in LA or go home to Chicago and my abusive mom."

I accepted Lola's story then, but now I needed to know the truth. "Lola, when the sheriff told us about the guitar player's death, you told us that the Lovey Dove Band disbanded after your mom died. That was the first I heard of her death. Now you say your mom is abusive and in Chicago. Which story is true? Is your mom alive or dead?"

Lola looked guilty because I caught her in a lie. "Yes, my abusive mom died just before I left Los Angeles. I didn't mention that because I didn't want pity. I just wanted to make it on my own, so I decided to return to Pittman because I was determined to connect to my roots in the Berkshires. It's where I spent many happy summers working as a teenager for Jana at Shakespeare and Company. Chicago holds no happy memories for me."

I filed this explanation away as a reminder to find out her mom's name and find her obituary. Over the last few years, Lola has been like a daughter to me. I love her flair for the dramatic, which isn't wasted on the preschoolers and their parents who frequent my store. Everyone loves Lola and will gather friends and relatives to bring their children to her storytelling events. The parents watch and listen just as enthusiastically as the children.

I can't believe Hollywood producers didn't grab her. She'd be great in dramatic roles, but comedy is her forte. I can see her as the next Bette Midler. Lola would be a great guest comedian at Sweet Indulgences' comedy night if Sadie takes my advice to institute a night for guest comedians to perform, but right now I am worried about Lola's possible connection to this murder victim, and her excuse for not telling us about her mother's death seems pretty lame. I wonder what Lola is covering up. I wonder why she never told me of her mother's death. What other secrets is she harboring?

Chapter 7

Disgusting Mopey Tyler

As I was wondering about Lola's connection to the victim, Sadie went to call Sheriff Houtman to see if he had returned to his office. The front bell of my Bookworm Shop jangled, and in walked Mopey Tyler, the disreputable owner of The Joker's Den.

When Sadie heard the bell, she immediately put the phone down before the line connected. Sadie saw him and cringed. He reminded her of the ISIS fighters who had tyrannized her neighbors, giving her terrible nightmares, and killed her brother Joseph. Every time Tyler saw her on Farley Square, he glared at Sadie with hatred. He was a pompous brute who thought he was so much better than others. He hated all immigrants, but since 9/11, Tyler felt he had a right to hate all Middle-Easterners, and he was determined to make Sadie pay for the sins of all terrorists.

Mopey Tyler is a crotchety, stuck-up man, who, as far as we know, has no family and is concerned with whatever is best for himself. The shop owners on Farley Square, a close-knit group, weren't sure how to handle his prejudicial, pompous, and hateful personality. If you say anything, Tyler says the opposite, and with such authority that you begin to doubt yourself. Not only is he rude to Sadie, but he also is rude to me because I am a businesswoman. Tyler looks down his nose at any woman who owns a business. This, obviously, doesn't sit well with our female merchants.

Tyler's shop, The Joker's Den, is disgusting, but he's more than disgusting. Favorite attire is a black suit that looks like an undertaker's outfit, and he sports a toupee on top of his balding head and dyed sideburns. He stares with a frown at anyone who comes into his shop, thus the nickname of Mopey.

My Bookworm Shop sits across from The Joker's Den, but sometimes I'm glad the street is wide enough to separate me from Tyler. I wonder if he ever was married and what his wife was like if he was. No one seems to know where he lived before appearing in Pittman. His entire background is a mystery, which a group of merchants is investigating. Tyler seems evil enough to be at the top of any murder suspect list.

The only two merchants that Tyler is friendly with are Mike's father, Sam, and Chester Fergusson, my next-door neighbor on Farley Square, who owns Welcome Realty, the company that sold Tyler The Joker's Den.

When I spotted Tyler entering my shop, I started toward him, watching him snarl when he spotted Billy on the floor snoring away. Sadie tried to shield Billy and steer Tyler to the other side of the shop but failed. I took a protective stance right in front of Tyler.

"Needed to add some sound effects to your quiet library-like store, George? You could try music." He expected Sadie and me to laugh at his weak joke. Tyler refuses to let anything go. He got right up in my face and demanded to know why a tramp was sleeping on my floor. "This is going too far, George. A tramp sleeping in your store? You are bringing down the standards of the Farley Square shops. We expect only the highest-class patrons to shop here."

I found myself wishing that my husband John were here. He wouldn't allow Tyler to insult me and denigrate my shop and customers. I could picture John physically kicking Mopey Tyler out of the store and running him out of town. "No one messes with the wife of a Navy Seal," John would say.

Snapping back to attention, I realized Tyler was still going on about the exacting standards that merchants must be held to and railing against my tramp. (I guess Billy has become my tramp as well as Sadie's, Lola's, Asher's, and Mike's.)

"Then why would we allow you to own a shop on Farley Square? You bring down our standards for decency," I muttered under my breath. To his ugly face I said, "If you don't like my customers, you can leave. I really don't need your business."

Tyler glared at Billy before turning to me. "You are probably harboring a criminal," he said in a derogatory tone. "This tramp could be the one who broke into my shop and wreaked havoc. He also could be a murderer. Have you heard about the body that kid Benny found this morning in the alley? No wonder this tramp is tired. He was up all night robbing the pharmacy, trashing my Joker's Den, and killing someone. I'm going to report this to Sheriff Houtman. He can knock some sense into you ladies."

I geared up to launch a tirade against this impossible man when Lola jumped in and said, "Why are you here, Mr. Tyler? May I help you select a book?"

"Farley Square is getting too dangerous. What with the robberies, murders, vandalism, and now tramps sleeping in what are supposed to be reputable stores. I need to get away from here. I need a long vacation. Do you have an atlas of South America and Central America? I also want travel books for the Islands in the Caribbean. I'm looking to take one fine trip very soon. Lola, do you think you can get together a package so I can plan my trip?" asked Tyler, all the while ogling Lola's fine figure.

I couldn't help myself. I retorted, "Why don't you just stay in South America? Farley Square would be better off without your risqué shop. We'd all welcome your departure. Go right ahead and report us to Sheriff Houtman. You can also mention to him that you can't keep your eyes off my clerk's body, you disrespectful little twerp." I normally like most people, but oh, how I hate this pretentious man. I also hated that he managed to kindle my anger.

Sadie looked like she was about to burst. Her face was red, and she had her hands balled up, ready to pounce on Tyler at any moment. I rushed to her and said, "It's okay, Sadie. We won't let anyone hurt you. You're in America now, and we protect our own."

As Sadie saw Tyler preparing to kick my sleeping tramp, she intervened, and said, "Tyler, don't you dare harm that young man. You touch him, and you'll answer to me, the sheriff, and all the merchants. We'll be glad to escort you to the nearest bus or plane as you leave this town forever. And speaking of tramps, Mr. Tyler, last week, I saw several unsavory types of people go into your shop and leave by the back door into the alley. Did you kick them out because they were tramps, or was there another reason for their sneaky behavior? Sheriff Houtman also questioned their presence when we spoke to him about it last week before the Farley Square Merchants' meeting. Those suspicious customers are probably the hooligans who trashed your shop and robbed the pharmacy. I suspect that you killed a customer because he wouldn't pay your prices or threatened to expose your drug dealing. That would account for the body in the alley behind your shop."

Tyler looked ready to kill Sadie. Convinced that the tramp sleeping on the floor was a criminal and that I was harboring him, Tyler started to speak and choked on his words because he was so mad. Sadie had hit too close to home. He prided himself on being regarded by all the Farley Square merchants as a brilliant businessperson with high morals even though we all suspected his morals were nonexistent. This tramp camped out on the bookstore rug, Tyler was sure, had no morals.

"Don't you ever accuse me of wrongdoing. I warn you, you foreigner, that no one gets away with accusing me of anything. Just watch your back," Tyler sputtered as he fled my shop.

"I think I've been threatened." Sadie laughed. "He thinks I could be afraid of the likes of him after all the carnage I've witnessed in Lebanon. Believe me, those ISIS followers knew how to frighten and threaten, and trust me, their threats were not laughable. I'm sure I've seen more murder than Sheriff Houtman will see in his lifetime. Don't worry, Robin. I am not intimidated by the likes of Mopey Tyler."

"Sadie, we need to let the sheriff know about Tyler's threat. He might actually try to hurt you."

Sadie said, "Robin. I'm quite able to take care of myself. I bought a gun and practiced shooting it as soon as I got to Pittman. No ISIS immigrant or Mopey Tyler will have a chance to hurt me." She smiled at me, and I believed her.

Lola, standing at the cash register, looked like she would like to throw the cash register out the door and smash Tyler with it. She was very protective of Sadie, who treated her with extreme kindness, and Lola felt sorry for Billy who seemed so pathetic and lost as he slept soundly on the rug. Lola remembered times, in her younger years, when she had to sleep anywhere convenient to be far away from her druggy mother. Billy reminded her of sad times as she grew up and of scary times in Chicago, one of which involved the Lovey Doves' Bluegrass Band.

Shaking off her unwelcome memories of drug-crazed stalkers and her mom's involvement with them, Lola spouted, "That Tyler is so horrible. I would bash that greasy toupee into his bald head if I wouldn't be arrested. We need to get rid of him."

The boys returned just as Tyler was fleeing out the front door. All of us ran to the window to see where Mopey Tyler had fled. He was marching down Farley Square stomping his feet and banging his fists together as he muttered to himself.

"He doesn't even know how to march," said Mike.

"Stomp, stomp, wrong. Heel, toe, step to the rhythm, much better," said Asher. "Tyler would never make it in marching band."

"I'm glad you boys can laugh and criticize his marching prowess, but we'd better warn Billy to stay away from Tyler's shop. Tyler won't have any qualms about doing Billy harm," I said.

Asher and Mike were excited. "This will wake Billy." They went to the book corner and began banging on a toy drum using a steam shovel shaped like the one in *Mike Mulligan and His Steam Shovel.* Not their best idea, and even the loud banging failed to rouse Billy.

"Boys, stop that noise right now. Do you want Mr. Fergusson from the real estate office next door to complain again about noise?"Asher and Mike looked at me and slunk to the refreshment counter to get some cookies.

"I wonder why Billy is sleeping so soundly?" I asked. "It's almost as if he hasn't slept in days. I know teenage boys are deep sleepers, but Asher would at least wake up if I were banging a drum."

Knowing that Lola had run into some vile characters during her youth, I knew she had developed great insight into a person's character. I took her aside since the boys were occupied eating cookies, and asked, "Do you think that Tyler has a connection to the murder victim? He's certainly mean enough to murder someone, and he seems anxious to get out of town. Do you think he is capable of resorting to murder if someone crosses him?"

Lola looked a bit shaken and said, "I wouldn't be surprised if Tyler wasn't behind all this chaos."

"Then you better stay away from him. I don't like the predatory way he looks at you."

"He gives me the creeps when he stares at me like that. I promise to avoid Tyler and the Jokers' Den," said Lola as she remembered another man who gave her the creeps.

A couple of months ago, Sadie, Lola, and I had started secretly researching Mr. Tyler's background for the Farley Square Merchants' organization. We were trying to uncover what had to be a mysterious past life. One thing that made everyone suspicious was that Tyler appeared out of nowhere last year with enough cash to purchase the former gift shop on Farley Square. Of course, Fergusson was happy for the commission and didn't care that The Joker's Den would not fit in with the other shops in our community. We very much doubted that Fergusson ran any kind of background check on Tyler. Cozy Gifts had been a cute boutique that sold homemade crafts. In two weeks, Mr. Tyler turned it into a shop that sold questionable items that would make citizens of our small town of Pittman blush. It was a Den all right, a den of iniquity.

Right after Tyler opened the Jokers' Den, Asher and Mike snuck past Tyler's shop and peeked in the window. That day, two unshaven men were handing Tyler an envelope. He then went to a barrel in the back of the store and filled plastic bags with an unknown substance that looked like flour. What was in those bags, and why did the customers leave by the back door?

When the boys reported back to us on their snooping, Lola suggested, "I'm sure Tyler is dealing drugs." She continued, "I also observed customers entering his shop and secretly leaving by the back door while clutching a sandwich-sized plastic bag. I suspect that one or more low-life broke into The Joker's Den to steal drugs. Those bags could be filled with heroin. Tyler certainly brings down the standard of Farley Square businesses.

"I wouldn't put it past Tyler to hang out with someone like the character dressed in a T-shirt emblazoned with a Bluegrass band logo. Perhaps the murder victim was buying drugs from Tyler. Do you think Tyler will hurt you, Sadie, or hurt Billy? He frightens me." Lola looked ready to cry at any moment.

"Don't worry, Lola. Tyler will have the wrath of the Lebanese upon him if he messes with me. Tyler should be the one afraid, not me," said Sadie, shaking her fist in the air.

I so admire Sadie's courage. She was the backbone of her Aboud family. In Lebanon, while escaping ISIS, Sadie and her brother Joseph almost walked right into a roving patrol, but Sadie spotted them and quickly whisked everyone away from danger, hiding them in a thicket of olive trees. Unfortunately, a few weeks later, in a raid on their refugee camp, ISIS found her brother Joseph hiding under a cot and whisked him off to train him to be an ISIS fighter for their cause, and that was the last Sadie heard of Joseph until one of the refugees reported that Joseph had been killed because he refused to become a suicide bomber. Feeling responsible for Mike and now Billy would help to heal Sadie's heart since she was still grieving the loss of her brother.

Chapter 8

Here Comes the Sheriff!

We all turned as the front door opened with a much gentler chime than when Billy crashed in. Sheriff Mark Houtman smiled at all of us. Sadie looked at him, and I could see her swoon. Sadie is about ten years younger than I am, and because of the upheaval in Lebanon, she never married. I'm afraid her crush on handsome Sheriff Mark Houtman is becoming more intense. She seems enamored by him. I saw them both seated in a booth at Sweet Indulgences at about 3:00 the other day. They were eating chocolate croissants and talking. I hadn't seen Sadie or the sheriff smile like that in a long time.

Houtman nodded to Sadie, then looked like he was going to announce something to us. I thought, "Uh oh, Mopey Tyler probably reported the tramp." I quickly offered the semi-intelligent sheriff some hot chocolate and steered him to the front counter away from the children's room, hoping he wouldn't hear Billy snoring away.

Distracted from his purpose and by Sadie, who often flirted with him, Sheriff Houtman teased Sadie. "Did you come over to get some good hot chocolate instead of that thick coffee you make at the bakery? I could sure use some of your delicious cookies, though, to go with this." Sadie blushed. She was mesmerized by the tall bachelor. If he doesn't appreciate her, he sure appreciates her cooking.

Sheriff Houtman turned to me and said, "My clerk tells me you might have some information about the murder."

Suddenly, Houtman stopped talking and jerked his head up. "What is that growling sound? Either your stomachs are craving cookies more than I am, or there's a bear loose in your back room."

As the sheriff turned to investigate, I tried to think of a plausible explanation. Sadie, as usual, was much quicker. "I just bought a new coffee pot for Robin as a birthday present for her fortieth birthday, and the directions say that it will make strange noises the first few times that we make a brew. They weren't kidding, were they? If the growling doesn't stop by our fifth attempt, I am going to return it."

Sheriff Houtman didn't believe Sadie's bizarre explanation, but he had learned to expect anything from Sadie and me, so he said goodbye and was about to leave when he stopped. "You told my clerk that you had information about the murder behind the Jokers' Den. What information do you have? You haven't seen any suspicious characters around here, have you?

"Also, there was some vandalism on Farley Square. Do any of you know anything about last night's vandalism of Klette's Pharmacy and The Joker's Den? Klette's Pharmacy was broken into, and cash was stolen. The cases behind the counter were smashed, and some drugs were taken while other stock was scattered all over the floor. The Joker's Den was also trashed. All the drawers in the back room were open, and contents were tossed all over, as well. Tyler is still taking inventory to see what might have been taken. Mr. and Mrs. Klette are so upset they couldn't open the pharmacy today."

"I don't know what you think we know," said Asher, "but we don't have a clue what happened."

"You might also be interested to know that Benny, a fellow member of your high school band, discovered the body in the alley. Do any of you boys or the rest of you have an idea who the victim is?"

"No clue," said Asher and Mike.

The sheriff glowered at them. "Deputy Murphy and I have never seen him before and have no idea who murdered him. Would you all look at these photos to see if you recognize the victim? We took these pictures at the crime scene and have sent them to the media and various police departments, hoping someone will recognize him.

Each shop's glass door was shattered. There were no fingerprints. We're trying to determine if the break-ins and vandalism were just mischievous pranks, a search for drugs, or if they are connected to the murder victim. We don't know if we're looking for one person or several. I heard about a vagrant in your store. Mr. Tyler is convinced he's the culprit. Is that the information you had for me?" The sheriff was clearly frustrated, or he wouldn't have revealed the details of the crime to us since he considered us just meddlers.

"Sheriff, do you think Tyler could have murdered the man?" I asked.

"No. Tyler says that you are harboring a tramp who may have committed these crimes and that Sadie is probably the tramp's accomplice." Sheriff Mark

Houtman glanced at Sadie, anticipating that being called an accomplice by the likes of Tyler would get a rise out of her.

Sadie didn't disappoint him. She piped up angrily, "Maybe Mopey Tyler was stealing drugs from Klette's Pharmacy to sell to the disreputable people who leave his shop each day with plastic bags filled with something suspicious. If Tyler decided to stage a break-in at his own shop to blame someone for the missing drugs from Klette's, he is your murderer. How dare he blame me. He is the most hateful person."

I broke into Sadie's tirade. "Plus, did you know that Tyler is planning quite the trip? He was in here today and purchased maps of Central and South America and travel guides. Maybe he needs the money from the pharmacy to fund his trip. Do you suppose he has to flee the country so he's not accused of murder, or does he have so much drug money that he must take a trip to establish offshore accounts? Did you know Mopey Tyler threatened Sadie and called her a disgusting foreigner?"

"Yes," said Sadie. "Who does he think he is threatening me? He doesn't know who he's dealing with."

"Funny you should blame Tyler, Sadie, since his justification for accusing you is because of your hot temper and exposure to violence when you lived in Lebanon. He said that you threatened him this morning. I can't imagine you had anything to do with any of these crimes, but you do seem to have a dislike of Tyler, so I can't disagree with him about your hot temper."

"Tyler said that I threatened him? You must be

kidding. He told me to 'Watch my back.' There's a threat if I ever heard one," said Sadie. She held her head up and looked defiantly at the sheriff determined that he wouldn't see her cry.

Sheriff Houtman stared at his shoes, looking guilty that he almost made Sadie cry. He had to admit that Sadie generated strange feelings in him every time he saw her. He sympathized with her hard life and escape to this country, and he admired her courage. She was the first woman who had attracted him since his wife died. Sadie was so different from his deceased wife, Grace, who was a shy, artistic type. Whenever Sadie challenged him or others, he was speechless. He pictured her as a warrior queen.

"That doesn't sound like a coffee machine to me," said the astute sheriff.

Sadie jerked her head up and looked at me. I shrugged. "Maybe it's Lola telling a story about a bear?" As usual, my explanation was weak so Houtman didn't believe a word I said. He turned and headed to the sound coming from the story corner. He stopped, stared, and then walked in a circle around the snoring Billy.

Houtman glared at us as we cowered next to the stage. "I don't suppose this is your coffee machine. Is this the person you told my clerk about? It looks a lot like the tramp that Tyler suspects of robbing Klette's Pharmacy or worse."

Of course, Billy chose that minute to wake up. He rubbed his eyes, then stretched out like a monkey, scratched his head, and said to Sheriff Houtman, "Who are you?"

"I could ask you the same question, young man,"

said the sheriff. "You better come with me. We need to take a trip down to the station. I have some questions to ask you. You have appeared in our town at a very unfortunate time."

Sadie jumped and rushed toward Houtman. I had to hold her back as she asked, "Are you arresting Billy just because of Tyler's say so? Look at him. He's just a poor kid. If you have questions, ask them now right here while he's surrounded by people who care about him. Robin didn't call to report a murderer, just to make you aware that we found a homeless young man in need of help."

Houtman was taken aback by Sadie's vehement, aggressive side. "Okay, okay, Sadie," he said. "I'll take the boy into Robin's office and question him if that suits you better. I don't understand why you are so worked up. Didn't you just meet this young man? How do you know what he has or hasn't done?" The sheriff went over to Billy and gestured for him to get up and come with him to the station.

Billy shook his head and ran his fingers through his shaggy hair. "*Why?*" he asked. "I didn't do anything wrong." Billy looked worried as the sheriff took him to my office in the rear.

Sadie glared at Sheriff Houtman as he led Billy into the backroom to interrogate him. We settled in to wait to see what the sheriff would do. Sheriff Mark Houtman and I had a history, and not a very pleasant one. When he came to Pittman from Boston, he thought he would have an easy job. He was tired of bureaucracy and violence. As a widower, he hoped to find someone with whom to share his lonely life. He was handsome, intelligent, and sexy, but he had the annoying habit of always thinking he was right. Also, he didn't respect the opinions of those who didn't agree with him, especially me. Only his opinion seemed to matter, even if he formed that opinion hastily. I was quick to rule out any relationship with the eligible bachelor except that of an adversary. I wasn't so sure about Sadie. She often became very shy when Houtman appeared and blushed after talking to him. Mark Houtman, for his part, seemed interested in both Sadie's past and present.

Chapter 9

Conspiracy

After questioning Billy, Sheriff Houtman set out to further investigate the break-ins and murder. He nodded to Sadie and me as he left my office but didn't say a word about his interrogation of Billy. Why wouldn't he at least tell us if he thought Billy was innocent or guilty before he rushed to leave?

Just then, the door flew open, and in rushed Chester Fergusson from Welcome Realty next door. He came in screaming, "I am tired of all the noise from this store. Doors banging, people shouting, and drums beating. How do you expect me to get any work done?"

Fergusson is a weasel of a man with the look of a cougar about to pounce on its prey. He continued to yell. "I have very classy clients who don't want to be interrupted as they discuss expensive real estate transactions."

Like classy clients would deal with a despicable person like yourself.

Fergusson stopped cold when he saw Sheriff Houtman standing to the side of the door he had just banged in. "Just the man I need to talk to. What are you doing about the reported possible arson at the pharmacy early this morning?"

"Arson?" said Sheriff Houtman. "As far as I know,

it was just a break-in. Where did you hear about arson?"

Fergusson said, "Mr. Klette from the pharmacy told me that his wife found matches in the back-storage room and several candles. She never saw them before, and she suspected that the vandals lit the candles, hoping they would start a fire in the storage room after they left."

"Arson, break-ins, and now, according to Tyler, harboring tramps," Fergusson said as he glared at Billy. "This neighborhood is a mess. Sheriff, before you run out of here, can you do anything about this disruptive noise from the Bookworm Shop? You are supposed to be the law enforcement liaison with the Farley Square merchants."

The sheriff, losing his normally calm demeanor, confronted Fergusson. "Are you aware that someone was murdered last night? Not only are we investigating a murder, but we also are looking for a vandal and a robber. I suppose you think a little noise is more important than all that. You are a self-centered so and so."

Flustered, Sheriff Houtman turned around and said to the rest of us, "I'll get back to all of you later. One crime at a time. I better get back to the station and check out this rumor of arson. I'll see what my deputy found out." Houtman then rushed for the exit.

Wow, he really went off on Fergusson. I wonder why. But the sheriff is a coward to just leave without even a comment about Billy's interrogation. I'm worried that he's already tried and convicted Billy in his own snap-judgement mind.

Fergusson shouted at Sheriff Houtman's fleeing

figure. Fuming, the arrogant man left the shop, banging the door behind him.

Billy came back with his head down and his hands stuffed in his pockets. Gone was his cocky attitude. Whatever Houtman said to him seemed to have broken his spirit.

"I'm really sorry, Ms. George, that I crashed through your door and made such a commotion," said a subdued-looking Billy.

Worried, Sadie went to Billy, and they found a secluded corner of the store to sit and talk. At least he seemed to be open to Sadie's questioning. He answered her questions while hanging his head and keeping his eyes downcast. I wondered what he was telling her about the interrogation.

When Billy went back to the Story Corner to collect his things, I asked Sadie, "Did Billy tell you what questions the sheriff asked? He seems deflated."

"No, and I didn't want to push him," Sadie said, "but Billy is going to stay at my house for a few days in case Tyler decides to seek revenge on me. Billy can help protect me and witness any verbal attack by that man."

I was surprised at Sadie's offer to have Billy stay with her. Sadie was always so independent. She never showed fear or accepted help. This report of someone offering money to find out her whereabouts had spooked her. I know she was feeling safe from ISIS here in our small town, but at this point, I wasn't sure if Sadie or Billy needed more protection. Maybe having Billy stay with her is a smart idea, even though she was trying to show the boy that not everyone suspected him.

"Billy," I asked, "should we contact any relatives

to tell them you're staying with Sadie?" I didn't want to be responsible for a runaway who happened to land in my shop, so I needed to try to find out where this stranger came from, and who was responsible for him. I also needed to ascertain if he could be a danger to Sadie. She was too trusting.

Just as I asked this, Billy spotted Asher and Mike, and perked up. "Hi, guys. What are you doing here?" When Asher told Billy that the Bookworm Shop was owned by his mother, Billy looked stunned, but he recuperated fast. He turned to me with his overconfident smile returning. "Oh, don't worry about me, Ms. George. My parents work long hours, and they don't mind if I sleep over somewhere. They'll be glad that I'm helping Sadie. I'll call and leave them a message," he said with a challenging look.

I wondered why Billy looked so guilty, and why I didn't believe him. I became more uncomfortable with this arrangement of Sadie's and meant to tell her this. She thinks she is invincible, but what if she'll be harboring a fugitive, or worse, a violent person sent by ISIS. I didn't yet have confidence that we should trust Billy, at least not one hundred percent. I know Sadie has a soft spot for vulnerable young people, but we know nothing about this strange young man. Also, now that arson had entered the picture, I remembered that Sadie found matches in Billy's pocket. He might not be as innocent as she thinks.

I pulled Asher aside and asked him about Billy's parents. "Another mystery, Mom. No one has seen his house or his parents. When Mike asked him what his parents did for a living, Billy changed the subject. When the band director asked if Billy's parents would be at the competition, he said they had to work, and again changed the subject. He's an expert at deflection. He'd make a great spy like 007."

"Did he ever say anything about an Aunt Dehlia," I asked, remembering his outburst at Story Hour.

"No, he refuses to talk about himself or his family, even to us, his closest new friends," said Asher. "We've tried to find out where he came from and where he goes each night, but we decided friends need to respect their friend's privacy. He's hiding something, but he doesn't want to open up to anyone yet."

Grateful that my son was always eager to talk about family or just about anything, I gave Asher a hug. "I hope you know you are always loved. I only hope that Billy is also loved. Let me know if he reveals anything about his family."

Chapter 10

Sadie's New Boarder and Protector

Since coming to our small town, Sadie had marveled at the number of books in our local library. In Lebanon, after ISIS terrorized her village, any books were either hidden away by the residents or destroyed by the wandering marauders. Saturday afternoon, Sadie and I set out to do more research at the library. As we were walking, I broached the subject of her new boarder. "Did Billy tell you anything about his family? I wonder where his parents are. The sheriff found matches at the pharmacy. I'm worried that those matches could be the ones you found in his pocket. Do you think there's a chance Billy started the fire at Klette's Pharmacy? He innocently broke into sleep there, and maybe lit a candle which caused a fire?"

"Don't worry so, Robin. Billy is a sweet kid. He just needs tender, loving care. You should have seen him eat dinner. It seemed like he hadn't eaten in days. I asked him when he last ate, but he laughed and said, 'Everyone says I have a hollow leg because I have such a hearty appetite.' He evaded my question.

"After dinner, we played Monopoly and talked. Billy told me about how he missed his grandparents. They were special to him. He lived with them for a while, but he didn't say why he left, or where they lived. He didn't say if his parents also lived with the grandparents. In fact, he didn't talk at all about his parents. Every time I brought up the subject, he would start getting excited about something else. I know Billy has problems, but I didn't want to lose his trust by pushing him to talk. One thing he did say that intrigued me was that an aunt also lived in his grandparents' house with them. This aunt used to read fascinating books or tell amazing stories to him every night. I wonder if that aunt could be his Dehlia?"

"Perhaps," I said.

"After the Monopoly game, we had some chocolate mint ice cream. I did ask Billy about the book, *Fire, the Hiccupping Dragon*, that he was excited about at Story Hour, but he got all secretive and said he might know the author. I think Billy not only might know the author, but my guess is that the author is a close friend or relative, maybe this mysterious aunt. What do you think, Robin?"

"Well, he had a very fond feeling for Fire. His emotions couldn't just be about a fictional dragon in a children's book. There must be a reason for his extreme behavior. Maybe the author was one of his parents or grandparents, or, as you guessed, the author was his Aunt Dehlia. The author is listed as Dehlia Woods. What about the picture in his locket? Did you ask him who it is? Could it be Aunt Dehlia? She looks much younger than the author's picture on the back of the book, though there seems to be a similarity."

"I didn't want to ask too many questions, or he might have gotten spooked and clammed up again."

"You're right. Billy seems jumpy but try to get some more answers. We need to know who is responsible for him. He's underage so we can't just keep him at your house. If Sheriff Houtman finds out he's staying there, he could call Children's Services, and we could get in trouble.

"Keep asking him questions and let's sort this mystery before the sheriff gets too suspicious. I don't like secrets when they involve vulnerable young men. Also, ask him about the picture in the locket and the key we found in his pockets. The more I think about it, I'm sure it's a safe deposit key. I mean, why would a teenage boy carry around a safe deposit key? We must be open to the fact Billy could have committed these crimes. Could the safe deposit box be where he stashes the money and goods he steals, if he is the thief?"

"No, I'm sure he isn't a thief. There must be some other explanation," said Sadie. "If he set the fire accidentally, he might not even realize it. He's too good of a kid to be a vandal or a thief, and certainly not a murderer."

"Mike and Asher are wondering about Billy's financial circumstances. He seems to fit in with all the rich and middle-class kids in their school. His vocabulary is extensive, and his speech shows a high level of education, and wow, is he smart. However, he dresses like a bum. Seldom does he wear more than one T-shirt in a week, and all the time, he wears the same old ratty jeans. His hair is down to his shoulders, and no one is sure when he last had it cut. He doesn't smell, which is surprising, though the boys suspect he's showering in the locker room at school," I said.

"If Billy's grandfather was poor, maybe his parents were too, and if he's desperate for money, maybe he did have something to do with the theft at the Pharmacy."

That was a logical conclusion in my head.

Sadie just glared at me. No way was she going to believe that Billy was a thief.

"There's one other thing I need to tell you," Sadie said, "and I'm not sure if I should mention it to Sheriff Houtman. I looked out my living room window last night at about eight, and I saw someone who appeared to be hiding behind the tree across the street. When he saw me look in his direction, he ducked behind the tree. I could have sworn it was Tyler. About fifteen minutes later, I heard a car rev up, but it was too dark out for me to see if it was Tyler's. What do you think I should do?"

"I think Houtman will just dismiss it as a figment of your overactive imagination, even though he seems pretty protective of you. He's so fixated on Billy being the thief, and he believes whatever Tyler tells him. Let's have Lola and the boys team up and watch your house for the next few days to see if they spot anyone lurking in the shadows. Be careful, Sadie. We know nothing about Tyler. Out of the blue, he showed up in our town. He could be a dangerous character. He also has it in for Billy, so you might both be in danger."

I second-guessed myself. "Maybe you should mention the stalking to Sheriff Houtman. Since he's a bit sweet on you, I'm sure he doesn't want to see you in any danger. Why don't you mention it to him when he stops for coffee in the morning like he usually does? In a more relaxed atmosphere, he might not think we're snooping."

Just as I started to ask Sadie more questions, we arrived at the library. As we went into the research room, we saw Fergusson and Mopey Tyler huddled together like conspirators at a table. Sadie and I snuck up behind them and hid behind a bookcase. The library table next to them was covered with huge maps and stacks of addresses and pictures of homes for sale. As we concealed ourselves, I hoped to hear what they were plotting, but they were whispering.

I did manage to hear Tyler say to Fergusson, "My rich realtor friend from Chicago will be here this week looking to invest in cheap property and then flip it for a huge profit. She would be willing to buy up all the stores on Farley Square if she can get a cheap enough price." He gave Fergusson a high-five then he dropped his voice, and I couldn't hear the rest of it.

A few minutes later, Tyler adamantly spoke to Fergusson loud enough for us to hear. "Fergusson, it was brilliant of you to stage the robbery. No one will ever suspect you, the upright and honest shopkeeper. They also won't suspect me no matter how awful they think I am. It was a stroke of genius to have my store vandalized. If you can scare Mr. Klette and his wife into selling the pharmacy, we'll have a good chunk of real estate on Farley Square. They're retired and just wanted to continue the legacy of Mr. Klette's dad who owned the pharmacy for twenty-five years, but his dad died last year. I'm sure that after the robbery, the Klettes won't want the added tension caused by the fear of burglars. They'll be anxious to sell and at a low price. Don't forget any profit you derive from these referrals; you owe me thirty percent. The only glitch in our buyout plan was the murder of that vagrant. Fergusson, tell me you had nothing to do with the murder," pleaded Tyler.

Fergusson's lips tightened, eyebrows pulled down

as he hissed, "I could ask you the same thing, Tyler. How dare you suggest that I'm a murderer. Did you murder the victim in the alley over drugs? You need to assure me you had nothing to do with the vagrant's murder. You don't trust me. I may not trust you either."

"Wow," Tyler said. "It looks like we both have trust issues."

Chapter 11

Chester Fergusson, owner of (Un)Welcome Realty

After witnessing Fergusson's angry exchange with Tyler, it confirmed for us that Fergusson was not the honest, friendly realtor he pretended to be. I knew this from our confrontations about noise at Story Hour, but Sadie, ever the optimist, had doubts. She was swayed by Ferguson's charm, and since he didn't have kids of his own, she just thought he might not be crazy about kids.

Dressed in pricey suits and impeccably groomed, we knew Fergusson only catered to rich tourists wanting to find a vacation home in the Berkshires. The only person he seemed friendly with was Mopey Tyler. Their friendship made no sense, and there the two of them were whispering together like long-lost friends, friends who also have heated arguments as they concoct their evil plans.

Because he was getting rich off the summer trade, Fergusson wanted nothing to do with the locals. He looked down his nose at the residents, particularly my customers. Several of them, who had growing families and needed bigger houses, had approached Mr. Fergusson to have him help them find a larger home in Pittman. Fergusson refused to work with them, and if he deigned to show them a property, it was usually rundown and not at all what they needed for their children.

Word had gotten out about his prejudice against large families and residents so they often just ignored (Unwelcome) Realty Company and found a friendlier realtor in Lennon, the next town over. Fergusson felt no need to cultivate local clients. He was satisfied with the tourists and rich clientele who came to town. The friendship between Fergusson and Tyler seemed sinister to me. Why was Ferguson befriending and meeting with the one disreputable shop owner? Could he know Tyler from previous dealings?

Last month, on behalf of the Farley Square Merchants' Association, I reported Fergusson to the authority, but Sheriff Houtman refused to investigate our complaints about Fergusson trying to buy up property from residents who were down on their luck and then reselling at a highly inflated price. This practice was driving up prices and making many areas of our town unaffordable for most locals. Sadie and I suspected Fergusson currently was trying to drive out kind Mr. Klette, thus the break-in at his pharmacy. Klette's Pharmacy was in a perfect spot for a high-end merchant to open a store to cater to the rich clients Fergusson hoped would buy up the properties in Farley Square. There was talk of expensive condos being built near Berkshire Park and even over the many shops on Farley Square. These potential shoppers would be drawn to high-end stores.

Now that these crimes have taken place, Sheriff Houtman doesn't seem to care about the merchants' complaints. He dismisses Fergusson as a suspect. He seems too fixated on Billy as the culprit to entertain the possibility of any other suspects. I'm beginning to think of Mark Houtman as Mr. Avoidance.

When Sadie and I went back to my bookstore Sunday night to relax with coffee, pastries, and a friendly chat, Lola was there catching up on the inventory. "Lola, this is your one day off. Why are you here on a Sunday?"

"I needed a quiet place to think, and I'm behind on your inventory," said Lola. I didn't quite buy her excuse, because I watched as she snuck peeks at us several times like something was on her mind. Either that or this arson and murder had me riled up to the point I suspected everyone.

Sadie and I told Lola about Tyler and Fergusson whispering in the library research room. Lola begged us to let her do some investigating on her own. We agreed, though we so distrusted Fergusson that we were a bit fearful for her safety. Then again, we did hear him tell Tyler that he had no connection to the murder. But if he were connected, Lola could be in danger.

Lola assured us that her acting ability would completely fool Fergusson, so we gave her the okay with the caveat that she should be sure Sheriff Houtman doesn't find out. He won't appreciate any detective work conducted by anyone other than his department.

****

Lola decided on Monday that she would approach both Fergusson and Tyler, saying she needed some part-time work to supplement her income from the bookstore. She wore her fanciest outfit and went next door on her lunch break. She was determined to get this role right and prove herself to Robin and Sadie. If she managed to get Fergusson to hire her, she will plan how to get Tyler to also give her a part-time job.

Lola entered Welcome Realty. "Mr. Fergusson, your realty company is so classy," Lola flattered him. "I heard that your secretary left, so I'm sure you can use a top-shelf receptionist. My shorthand is rusty, but I'm an excellent typist and am great with people. My winning personality has been an asset at the Bookworm Shop. Though I have been working there for awhile now, I see no room for advancement or any chance to better myself if I stay there. Would you consider hiring me part-time on a trial basis? I've done quite a bit of customer service and would be an asset to your company. Plus, I know many of the movers and shakers in the area, both locals and those summer tourists from New York and Boston in particular. This familiarity would be a boon for your real estate business."As she said this, Lola flaunted her beauty, determined to infatuate Fergusson.

Fergusson stared at her new and up-front transformed self. She ignored the way he leered at her from head to toe, which gave her the creeps. But she was on a mission.

Lola had made sure to add keywords in her pitch to be hired, words that would spark enough interest to hire her.

About a minute later, he nodded and smiled. "Sure Lola, I'm willing to give a beautiful, smart woman like you a trial as my receptionist. I also have several high-end clients that I am sure you could service. How about starting Monday morning from nine to twelve? By the way, are you also available in the evenings for client meetings?" he asked.

"I'm not sure about the evenings yet, but I'll see you from nine to twelve each weekday, I work at the bookstore from one to seven so that should work out," said Lola, trying to hold back the smirk she felt coming on. The evening hours concerned her, but she'd let Robin know.

****

Lola reported back to me that she was now a part-time receptionist for Fergusson.

"Fergusson also referred to having a night job for me, servicing high-end clients. I wonder what type of services he wants me to offer. You don't suppose he and Tyler work together trafficking drugs and prostitutes, do you? I wouldn't put it past that shady pair," Lola said with a perplexed frown.

Sadie and I agreed that not only does Lola need to spy on Fergusson's real estate business, but she needs to be a fly on the wall, probing into the machinations of his side business. Because Lola's acting ability seems so convincing, we also agreed that she should try to get a part-time job at Tyler's Joker's' Den on Saturdays.

Lola agreed. "I'll check with Tyler tomorrow and see if he needs any extra help. A short skirt will definitely be part of my costume. Tyler seems susceptible to the charms of a beautiful woman. Rumor has it that he often tries to hit on any pretty woman who enters his shop."

Now I prayed Lola would be strong enough not be swayed by any of Tyler's evil dealings.

Chapter 12

Investigator Lola

Lola's first day on the job at Welcome Realty, she confirmed that what Robin and Sadie thought they overheard was true. As Lola was getting some supplies, she found a list of potential clients and a map of all the shops on Farley Street. She stuck the incriminating documents into her huge pocket. When she went to lunch, she got a sandwich and went to a hidden bench in Tanglewood Park. She took out the documents and read the elaborate plans. Fergusson intends to buy up cheap property from the poor residents of Pittman and resell it to high-end clients for housing. He is hoping to buy up all the stores on Farley Square to expand his realty company and then sell the other stores to whoever would pay the highest prices. Tyler's aunt was listed as a potential buyer.

As she read these documents, Lola had a hard time appreciating the beauty of Tanglewood because of Fergusson's evil plan to ruin their quiet little town. She mulled over his plan as the beautiful music came from the bandstand where the Boston Symphony Orchestra was practicing for next week's concert. How she wished she could just lie back on a blanket and enjoy the wonderful music filling the green lawn. The orchestra was practicing for the production of "West

Side Story." The orchestra was going to play the music while the film was showing on the big screen. "Oh, to be carefree and innocently naïve," sighed Lola.

When she returned from lunch, Lola snuck back into the supply room and managed to slip the documents back into the file just as Fergusson came looking for her. She couldn't let him get away with destroying the whole culture of their town. She had seen enough schemes and destruction in her life. Sadly, she remembered her mom's path to destruction when she sang in Lovey Doves' Bluegrass Band. Her mom loved the limelight of performing on stage. Customers loved her sweet, strong voice as she would belt out song after song. Unfortunately, along with fame came money and the opportunities that money can buy. At first, her mom only tried uppers to make her feel more energetic as she performed night after night. But then she tried harder drugs mixed with alcohol. This addiction led to her downfall and eventual death. Lola will never forgive whoever sold her mom those drugs, and she was determined to never follow in her mom's footsteps and give in to this destructive behavior.

Ferguson interrupted her sad reminiscences. "Lola, there you are. Are you free Friday night? I'd like you to meet Mr. Boswell. He's a very rich client looking to invest in property here in Pittman. I think he would enjoy having dinner with you. What do you say?" asked Fergusson.

"Well, Mr. Fergusson, I'm sorry. Maybe another night. I have an engagement I can't break for Friday night." Fergusson's eyes swept the office as Lola spoke. Was that file cabinet drawer partially open? He was always careful to close each drawer when he used the file. Lola quickly turned toward the file cabinet and said, "I better get those files straightened out so I still have a job to come back to. I left the file drawer open so I could easily remember where to return the files from my desk that I was organizing. Everything is so helter-skelter in some of those files."

She felt his suspicion rising. *Is he on to me?*

Lola left a frustrated Fergusson glaring after her as she went to get the files off her desk.

Chapter 13

Lola Reports Back

Monday night, when Lola gave me the report of her findings on Fergusson's plan to flip properties, I realized that he had a strong motive for the robbery of Klette's Pharmacy and even the vandalism in Tyler's shop, though I wondered why he would trash The Joker's Den since Tyler seemed to like his friend. I also wondered how Fergusson could be connected to the murder victim.

I told Asher and Mike about Fergusson's scheme to flip cheap property, and the boys decided to try and foil Fergusson's real estate deals.

Tuesday, they went into Fergusson's Realty and Mike said exactly what we discussed. "Mr. Fergusson, I have a rich aunt who wants to move here to mother me because my dad is always so busy. You'll love my Aunt Tillie. She comes from Detroit, Michigan, and wants to buy a house here in Pittman. Her Grosse Pointe mansion on Lake Shore Drive was so big and so beautiful, it would be hard to match here in the Berkshires. I told her the only one who could find her a house similar to that one was you, Mr. Super Real Estate Agent. Her house was on Lake St. Clair and had a view of the lake. On a clear day, you could see right across to Canada. That beauty sold for over two million dollars. What do you think, Mr. Fergusson? Do you think you can find her a similar house here in old Pittman, gateway to the Berkshires, maybe with a lake view?"

The kids in the band looked up to Mike because he could weave the most fantastic stories or lies ever. That's how he got the nickname Pinocchio. My son, Asher, had gotten into quite a bit of trouble over their last big venture into untruths.

Mike related to me how Mr. Fergusson was all smiles, and said, "Of course, I can find a house for your aunt, Michael. Have her call me as soon as she gets into town. I'll start lining up properties to show her."

I was pretty sure dollar signs danced through Fergusson's head as Fergusson imagined the money he would earn by selling properties to Tyler's real estate broker and Mike's Aunt Tillie. The man, from what we had overheard, was determined to sell all the stores on Farley Square as he got rid of each owner.

****

After thanking Ferguson, the boys tried to smother their laughter.

"What a jerk," Mike said once they left Welcome Realty. Now, they needed a grand plan, a plan to make Mr. Fergusson so nervous that he would sell his own shop to their friend, Wayne, the bike man, who was eager to open a shop on Farley Square.

"At least Wayne will not tell your mom to keep the children quiet who come to her shop. Let's team up with Lola to make Fergusson go away," said Mike.

The boys' plan would depend on Lola's acting skills and her mastery of disguise. She agreed to impersonate Aunt Tillie and meet with Fergusson. The boys were confident Lola could pull off this deception. She'd have to be a superb actress to keep Fergusson from recognizing her since she now worked part-time for him. Lola assured the boys that Fergusson would never recognize her impersonation of an elderly rich client. She told them when she took acting at Dartmouth, she had a class in the art of disguise and deception. She got an A in the difficult course.

Before band practice Tuesday afternoon, Asher laughed as Mike imitated Mr. Fergusson to the tee. "Of course, I can find a house for your aunt," he sputtered, spitting out each word in just the right Fergusson tone.

Billy heard their laughter as he took out his mellophone for marching band and stuffed his French horn into his band locker. He was becoming quite good at making the transition from French horn to the shorter, lighter-weight mellophone that was so much easier to carry when marching. By Spring, Billy should be a great help to the marching band as they competed for the State championship.

Billy asked the laughing pair, "What are you guys cackling about? You look like Mr. Lewis and Mr. Gant when they're mocking the principal. Are you mocking someone, or is something actually funny?"

Mike told Billy about their plan to drive Fergusson from the shops and replace his with a cool bike shop. They explained how Lola had agreed to impersonate Aunt Tillie, a rich client from Detroit. While talking to Billy, Mike and Asher hatched another part of their destruction plan. "While we are conning Fergusson," Asher said, "we should expand our plan to include Tyler. He's already spooked by the robberies and murder, so it shouldn't be too hard to spook him enough to drive him away, and his shop is right across the street from the realty office, a perfect place for Wayne's bike shop. Wayne could buy both shops and open one for repairing bikes and motorcycles and one as a retail showroom. Billy, we're putting you in charge of the Tyler Destruction Plan. See what you can dream up."

"Who's Wayne?" asked Billy.

Mike answered, "Wayne graduated last year. He's a whiz at fixing motorcycles, and he's always dreamed of opening a Fix-It shop for all kinds of bikes. His grandmother just died and left Wayne a lot of money. Wouldn't it be crazy if we can show him how much a bike shop is needed and suggest that Tyler might be willing to sell his Joker's Den? This would, of course, be after Lola and all of us work our destructive magic to make Tyler's shop disappear. A Fix-It Shop for bikes sure would be a better addition to the Farley Square Shops than a smut shop like The Joker's Den. Then, if Fergusson's plan of buying all the stores is thwarted, Wayne can also open a Bike Showroom in the Realty office next to my mom's shop. Parents who frequent the Bookworm Shop will be glad to have a local bike shop for their kids to select the perfect bike."

"I know how to fix every kind of bike," Billy said. "My granddad had a Harley and insisted that I learn where every screw was placed and how each part worked." For a moment, Billy looked like he might tear up. "My granddad was the best mechanic in our hometown. Everyone brought their cars and bikes to him. Mr. Clyde W. Woods could have been rich, but he refused to charge people more than they could afford, and since most of the customers in our hometown were poor, they couldn't afford to pay a lot of money for repairs. I really looked up to my granddad because of his kindness and his awareness of others' needs."

Billy snapped out of his melancholy and asked, "Do you think Wayne will give me a job in his shop when it opens? I sure can use the money." Billy blushed. Embarrassed, Billy headed for the door. "See you at band practice."

Once Billy left, Mike turned to Asher. "Did you realize Billy just told us his grandfather's last name? We can search for Clyde W. Woods and mechanic and find out more. Too bad we have no idea what town he lived in."

Right after band practice, Mike and Asher planned to warn Billy about Tyler's threat to Sadie, but after the last note was played, Billy rushed away. Mike called out and stopped him. "Wait, Billy. We need your help while you're staying at Sadie's house. Tyler has threatened to hurt Sadie. First priority is to make sure that you both are safe in case Tyler or Fergusson attempts to pull something shady. Sadie thinks that Tyler was watching her house a couple of nights this week. We're not sure why he was watching, but it looks very suspicious. Tyler hates Sadie. If it isn't Tyler watching, maybe someone from ISIS tracked her to this country. We need to keep our eyes and ears open for trouble."

Asher added, "While you're staying with Sadie for a few days, glance out the window as often as possible. If you see anyone who looks suspicious, call one of us immediately, and make sure Sadie stays away from the windows. You two shouldn't go out alone. We won't rest easy until something is done about Tyler, and we've eliminated anyone from her past life tracking her. Do you think that the same people who killed her brother Joseph could be out to get her?"

"I hope not," Billy said, his tone full of conviction. "Asher, I'll watch over Sadie. She's been really nice to me. She acts like a mom and seems to care about me. Does Tyler know I'm staying at Sadie's house? If not, Lola needs to tell him since she works at Welcome Realty and The Joker's Den part-time. I don't think Tyler will go after Sadie while I'm staying with her."

"I think Sadie misses her younger brother and sees you as someone like him to mother and keep safe. How long will you be able to stay with Sadie? Don't you have to go home soon? Won't your parents expect you?" asked Mike.

"No, I called them and explained why Sadie needed me to stay, and they okayed it. They've heard me talk about her, and they respect my insight into people. Anyway, see you all later," Billy hurriedly said.

"You guys should come over to my house tomorrow night after band practice," Asher said, "and we can finalize Lola's demolition plan for Fergusson and come up with a scheme to spook Tyler into selling to Wayne. Lola has agreed to be there. We can ask my mom if we can order pizza. Maybe Sadie will bring hummus and baba ghanoush with Syrian bread for snacks. MMMMM, my favorite snacks. The Lebanese sure know how to cook."

Mike and Billy nodded.

"Do you think we should let Sheriff Houtman know what's going on?" Mike asked. "If we're lucky, he'll see how clever our plans are and include us in his investigation, but he'll be furious if we interfere with his plans. I'll invite him over for dinner. I'll warn Lola that the accusatory sheriff might be there. We should at least let Houtman know that someone, maybe from ISIS, seems to be stalking Sadie. The Sheriff cares about her and that might make him willing to have our help."

"Sounds great. See everyone tomorrow night at the dinner party," said Billy.

When he left, Mike said, "Asher, in the meantime, let's see if we can track down Clyde W. Woods and find out Billy's grandfather's background and discover where Billy lived before he came to Pittman. Let's also find out more about Sadie's hometown in Lebanon and what happened to her brother Joseph. Maybe some people in the refugee camp or other Lebanese who came to the Northeast from Lebanon to stay with relatives will know more about who killed Joseph and Sadie's family, and whether ISIS is still looking for Sadie."

"I'll get right on it," said Asher. "I'll let you know tomorrow what I find out."

Chapter 14

Suspicions Revealed and Rebuked

Wednesday evening after dinner, where we stuffed ourselves on Sadie's appetizers and the pizza, the boys excitedly explained to Sheriff Houtman they heard that Fergusson was driving down the price of properties on Farley Square in order to buy up the stores and flip them for inflated prices to sell to some out-of-town people.

They told Sheriff Houtman this made them sure that Fergusson trashed Klette's Pharmacy and The Joker's Den to scare off the owners. Mike even suggested Fergusson was responsible for the murder of the man found in the alley, but they admitted they had no proof of any of these allegations.

No one wanted the sheriff to know Lola had raided Fergusson's files or that she was planning to impersonate a buyer. Mark Houtman would holler and forbid her from interfering in an ongoing investigation.

Sheriff Houtman frowned at the boys as he listened to their allegations, then he said, "If I catch any of you, and that includes the grownups in this room, inserting yourself into our investigation, I'll arrest you for obstruction of justice. We are looking for a murderer who is probably still right here in our town. It is too dangerous to be playing amateur detective. Do you understand me? Sadie, Robin, and Lola, this means you also."

We all looked guilty and nodded our heads. I'm pretty sure he didn't believe a thing we just reported. He then turned and left in a hurry.

Chapter 15

Aunt Tillie

Thursday morning, while working at Welcome Realty, Lola pretended to take a call from Michigan. She carried on a fake conversation with Mike's Aunt Tillie. When Fergusson's customer left, Lola went back to his office and reported, "Mr. Fergusson, I just took a call from a client in Michigan who wants to have you show her property in Pittman and Lennon. I didn't want to interrupt your important client meeting so I got her details for you.

"Tilly Marksman says she is Mike's aunt and will be coming to town this afternoon on the four o'clock train from New York for a quick overnight visit with Mike and his dad. I went ahead and made an appointment for you to take her to dinner and show her the specs for properties she might be interested in. According to Aunt Tillie, these properties must be 'cozy, lakeside, up-to-date, expensive and bring a substantial profit in resale.' If she picks one, you could show it to her tonight or early tomorrow morning before she returns to New York on the twelve-p.m. train. She has business to do there before she returns to Detroit. If that doesn't suit you, I can call her back to reschedule."

"No, that schedule is fine, Lola. You were right not

to interrupt my meeting. Go ahead and schedule this rich aunt of Mike's. He told me about her, and I'm eager to meet Aunt Tillie. I hired you for your efficiency, so never second-guess yourself. Thank you for taking care of this for me," Fergusson said.

Lola texted Asher and said she needed my help with adjusting her disguise. I agreed to meet her in Stockbridge at the Shakespeare Playhouse in the costume room at noon when I closed the bookstore for lunch. Lola had worked in the costume shop with her friend Jana before Jana died, so all the staff knew her and were glad to lend her clothes befitting a rich widow.

By the time Lola and I finished putting the finishing touches on her disguise. No one would ever recognize her as Lola, Pittman's actress in residence. We were sure that Fergusson would be none the wiser. Lola had to make sure she got to the train station before the 4:00 train arrived. In case Fergusson decided to check Aunt Tillie out before his dinner meeting, Lola wanted to be seen leaving the station and hailing a cab to Mike's house.

When Lola doddered out the door, flouncing the feathers on her wide-brimmed hat, I laughed and looked forward to her description of the deceptive caper. I went back to my shop picturing Lola and Fergusson together.

Friday afternoon, when Lola came to work, she brought lunch from Sweet Indulgences, and naturally, Sadie came to share not only lunch but the whole story of Lola's performance.

"You should have seen Fergusson gushing such politeness and compliments. You'd think I was royalty. We had an elegant meal at Mario's, then he produced about ten glossies of awfully expensive houses for sale in and around Pittman. After dismissing all houses in the mountains or city, we were left with three on a lake or in a beautiful rural setting." Lola continued relating this description of the venture. She told Fergusson, "I think I will rule out the rural home since I am a city girl born and raised. That leaves the two lake houses, but there is a problem with both. Though they seem very elegant, they both have steep staircases, and at my age, I need everything on one floor. One of the lake houses is one level, but I wouldn't want to walk down that uneven backyard to the lake."

When Aunt Tilly presented these problems to Fergusson, he was frustrated. He had counted on an instant and lucrative sale. "Perhaps I can get together a few more properties and meet you for breakfast tomorrow to go over their merits before you leave. If you like any of those properties, we can communicate by email and have a simultaneous showing and closure of the sale the next time you can get back to Pittman, or we can do all the details of the sale by email and Skype so the deal is closed, and the house is ready for you to enjoy when you next arrive in Pittman. You are welcome to have your lawyer join us on the video call at closing so you will feel confident that all the details are taken care of legally."

Aunt Tilly, playing the believable role of a doddering old woman, thought for a long time as Fergusson squirmed silently. Then she said, "I am sorry. I just feel so rushed. I must get back to New York on the noon train. I'll talk to my lawyer about everything when I get back to Grosse Pointe and contact you as soon as I make a decision. Thank you so much for all your trouble. I'm sure you understand my hesitancy to plow ahead without legal counsel since this is quite an expensive venture. Mike can give you all my contact information."

By the time Lola, aka Aunt Tilly, finished her tale, Sadie and I were laughing uncontrollably and couldn't wait to tell Mike and Asher. Not only was the story outlandish, but Lola's gestures, facial expressions, and accents were hilarious as she described the scene to us. She exaggerated her Chicago accent by drawing out her A's and made her eyelids droop and her lips quiver. Her face looked like a female Jim Carrey. Lola's reputation as a great actress was bolstered in our minds by this great performance.

Chapter 16

Amateur Sleuths Look for Motives

After my shop closed on Friday, I agreed to meet Sadie and Lola at Sweet Indulgences. We were huddled together in my favorite booth looking out on Main Street, savoring Sadie's melt-in-your-mouth chocolate chip cake. Drizzled with raspberry topping, this three-layer cake was a delight for anyone's taste buds.

I love Sadie's shop. She has the walls decorated with photographs of kids and adults eating every imaginable sweet treat. The funniest pictures are the ones of toddlers who don't quite get the ice cream to their mouths and end up with it smeared all over their faces. One wall holds a map of Lebanon with pictures of Sadie's family surrounding it. One photo shows Sadie holding her brother Joseph's hand as he looked up at her with the most adorable smile on his face. I see why she misses him so much.

The booths in Sweet Indulgences go around the room and are comfy mint green with white Formica tables. The front display case is filled with delicious-smelling cakes, brownies, and cookies. When the shop door opens, a tuneful chime plays as customers enter.

Sadie, Lola, and I were huddled near the big picture window looking out on Farley Square. I loved all the shop owners on Farley Square except, of course,

Ferguson and Tyler. Our mission right now was to figure out who had a motive for the murder, robbery, and vandalism.

Lola reported, "I think Fergusson is involved either in the vandalism or the murder. It must be either Tyler or Fergusson since they're the evilest people I know in Pittman. When Fergusson met with Aunt Tilly, besides showing her the most expensive properties around town, he also had a list of shops that he might be able to convince her to invest in. Aunt Tilly, alias me, just wasn't interested in commercial property. When I uncovered Fergusson's plot to buy up all the shops on Farley Square, I thought that might be a motive for the vandalism, but not for murder. I'm sure he is trying to scare off the shop owners with vandalism and violence. He seems anxious to get his hands on most of the shops. In his office, I found a list of every shop with the name of the owner, what the owner originally paid for the shop, and how much he/she is getting in rent. He also lists the owners' current financial status, their family situation, and possible ways to intimidate or put pressure on the owner. I copied just one page of his list of how to acquire the shops from their owners."

Fergusson's Intimidation List

Sweet Indulgences had Sadie's Aunt Florence listed as the owner, and the intimidation list included:

1. Degrade her niece in the eyes of the sheriff

2. Accost Florence or her niece at night as she leaves the shop

3. Hurt the tramp Sadie seems to care about

4. Insult Aunt Florence's family

5. Incite members of the town to think her niece is a terrorist, and Florence is harboring a terrorist

6. Incite members of the community to boycott her shop because she is a foreigner

7. Write a restaurant review of Sweet Indulgences that says how awful the food and service are

8. Plant rodent droppings in Sweet Indulgences and report it to the Health Department

This list was evidence that shows Fergusson also had a motive for stealing from Klette's Pharmacy to try to scare Mr. Klette into selling, and he could want to drive Tyler out also, though Tyler is his friend.

Lola also expressed my confusion. "I wonder why Fergusson would want to scare his friend, Tyler, and how is this connected to the body in the alley? Do you suppose the murder victim was a friend of Tyler's, and they were going to blackmail Fergusson and expose his sinister plan?"

"I'm not sure about the connection to the murder," Sadie said. "Fergusson seems too smart to do something so stupid and violent. If his threat against me and my aunt was to scare us enough to sell Sweet Indulgences to him, he has never dealt with anyone as stubborn as Lebanese women. No way will he ever get me to sell my aunt's shop to the likes of him. Wanting to monopolize all the shops on Farley Square does give him a strong motive for causing trouble for all of us. I wonder how much money he'll make if he manages to buy most of the Farley Square Shops, and I wonder if Tyler shares in any of Fergusson's profits since they seem so buddy-buddy lately."

"Tyler also has a strong motive," I chimed in. He might need the insurance money from the vandalism, or he might have stolen the drugs himself to collect the insurance and resell the drugs to some dealer, or the murder victim was one of the low-life characters who frequent The Joker's Den, or a dealer who wanted to extort more money from Tyler. We should examine their finances. I wonder if the sheriff has thought of this. It would be easier for Sheriff Houtman to get a warrant for Fergusson and Tyler's bank accounts than us. Sadie, you ought to suggest to the sheriff that he investigate their finances and give him a copy of the intimidation list. I'm sure the sheriff would not want any suggestions from me."

"And what makes you think he will want my suggestions?" said Sadie, blushing as she rolled her eyes.

"You know the sheriff has a crush on you, Sadie. If you don't know, we all do," I said.

Sadie looked down at the floor. "Robin, I haven't had a romance since I left my high school boyfriend in Lebanon. I've never heard from him since his family fled the country. I hope he got out safely."

"You know," interrupted Lola, "you've got a point about Tyler's friendship with Fergusson. Tyler might think he will get a cut of the money Fergusson makes if he sells off the shops. Tyler strikes me as a very greedy and conniving person who will stop at nothing, not even murder, to amass a large bank account."

"At the library, we did overhear Tyler and Fergusson talking about a thirty percent commission for Tyler on the properties he suggested. I'll ask the sheriff about the finances, but don't forget Mike's dad," said Sadie. "His Ten Pins Bowling Alley isn't doing very well. Mike said that Sam doesn't get many customers lately. It's no wonder if he is as surly to customers as he is to Mike. Sam might need money, so Fergusson hired him to commit the robbery and vandalize The Joker's Den. The murder victim could be an ex-con who served time with Sam or Frank, and had a beef with him, or was trying to blackmail Sam because of his parole violations. I don't know if Sam's capable of arson or murder, but his financial motive for some crimes seems solid. Sam does have a criminal record and did time in jail. He also isn't exactly sticking to the parameters of his parole.

"His employee, Frank, also served time with Sam. Maybe the victim was threatening Frank and Sam, and together they decided to eliminate the threat. We know little about Frank. Why was he in jail? What is his history? He seems like a likable guy, but we know nothing about his past."

"I've observed one thing about Frank," Asher said. "I've seen him stick up for Mike when Sam gets abusive and lashes out at Mike. I think highly of Frank for that gesture."

"Then there's Billy," said Lola. "Sheriff Houtman seems convinced Billy committed the crimes because he needs the money and wanted to steal the drugs from Klette's Pharmacy to sell at the high school. The fact that he just showed up two months ago out of nowhere could mean he was casing the places and decided to rob and vandalize the stores. If this theory is true, Billy could be casing our bookstore and Sadie's shop also."

At that point, Lola had to break the tension. She stood up and grabbed a throw from the couch. The throw became her cloak as she slunk around the room casing the joint, holding a ruler from my desk as if it were a gun. "Oooh, I'm on the prowl casing the joint, casing the joint. Oooh, hear me howl," she yelled, making us convulse with laughter. Then she switched gears and impersonated Sheriff Houtman. "Looking for clues. Is it you or you?" she chanted as she pointed the pretend gun at each of us.

"I really hope you make it on Broadway someday. Don't forget, we all get tickets to opening night."

Lola wore her serious face again. "I don't believe this theory that Billy is the main suspect, but Houtman does. Maybe that's why Houtman is so concerned. He knows Sadie cares about Billy, and he does have a soft spot for her. I just can't see Billy as a murderer."

Just as we were about to sum up, the bell on the door chimed, and in walked Sheriff Mark Houtman. Because he sort of slunk into the shop, we all cracked up picturing him as Lola's prowler and detective. He didn't quite know what to make of us. The look on his face told us he thought we were all going crazy. He strolled up to us, looked right at Sadie and me, and said, "Not trying to play detective again, are you, ladies? I hope I'm not interrupting your yack fest, but I need to question you all about a murder, robbery, and vandalism, and that's no laughing matter."

"We planned to share our findings with you the first chance we got. You must be clairvoyant, Sheriff, because here you are just in time." I wiped the smirk off my face, put on what I thought was my most innocent look, and invited him to join us. Sadie looked like she wanted to bolt.

"Sheriff, you're correct on one point. We *are* doing some detective work as we try to establish motives and share some of the information we've gathered. We are not meddling because we were just getting to the motives. If you want to quit mocking us and sit down, you might learn something."

Insulted but curious, Sheriff Houtman sat down.

"Okay, we decided that the suspects with motives are Fergusson, Sadie, Tyler, Billy, and Sam, Mike's dad," I summarized. "You can witness our vote to see if we, including you, all agree on the strongest candidate."

"Don't forget yourself, Robin, and Lola, Asher, and Mike," he said.

I just glared at him. "Okay, I stand corrected; the suspects with motives are Fergusson, Tyler, Sadie, Billy, and Sam, Mike's dad, and, according to Sheriff Houtman, we also need to add Mike, Asher, Lola, and myself, though I don't see any motives arising for his additions."

"Who do each of you vote for?"

"Fergusson," said Lola.

"Tyler," said Sadie.

"Sam," I said.

"Any of the boys, Billy, Asher, or Mike," said the Sheriff.

"Well, I guess we don't agree, except, the only people who think Billy is the prime suspect are Sheriff Houtman, Tyler, and Fergusson. Let's check them all out further," I said. "We'll compare notes at the barbeque tomorrow at Sadie's house."

Sadie turned to the sheriff. "Mark, do you think you could look into Fergusson and Tyler's financial situations by getting access to their bank accounts? On all the TV detective shows, you always hear, 'Follow the money.' I'm sure if anyone can find a financial trail, it would be you. I understand you are quite the whiz with a computer. Also, you haven't told us if arson was involved as reported by Fergusson."

Sadie must have felt bad taking advantage of the Sheriff's admiration of her, but Lola and I had requested her to ask him.

"There was attempted arson," said the sheriff. "We found evidence of a slight fire from the kerosene and ash in the backroom at The Joker's Den."

"Did you find the kerosene can? Were there any fingerprints on it?"

"I can't comment on an ongoing investigation. Also, do I need to remind you that this isn't some fictional crime show on TV, and you are not detectives? We are dealing with a murder, and I don't want any of you becoming the next victim. Leave the detecting to the professionals," he said as he stood to leave.

"Sheriff," I said, "we are having a barbeque tomorrow night at about six at Sadie's house. Would you like to join us? Sadie and I are going to do some research on Tyler and Fergusson in the morning at the library. We'll share the results of our research with you so you don't think we're keeping secrets. We also promise not to act on any information we may find."

"I'm holding you to your word. No meddling. No taking any chances. The boys already invited me, so I'll be there," he said as he left.

"Feel free to bring a dish or snack to share," I mischievously yelled as he took a step out the door. Might as well give him something to do rather than suspect us.

"Lola, could you please cover for me in the bookstore tomorrow morning? Myrna is covering for Sadie at Sweet Indulgences so we should have a good chunk of time to find out something about these secretive men. We'll fill everyone in on what we find

89

when we get to dinner tomorrow night.

"Though I invited him to the barbeque, I really don't want to deal with that irritating man, but it's necessary to get him on our side so that he starts looking at those who have motives other than Billy. The dense sheriff considers me a suspect and wants to test my candles for a match to the ash he found at the arson scene. He makes me so mad. Maybe if we have some facts to share with him, he'll fill us in on his investigation and quit treating us as suspects. Sadie, you'll need to be your most charming self to win him over to our side and get his mind off Billy."

I was a little worried when Sheriff Houtman mentioned the arson because I remembered that we found a pack of matches in Billy's belongings when he first crashed on my rug in the bookstore. If the sheriff finds out about the matches, he might jump to the wrong conclusion again.

Lola seemed a little edgy when I mentioned the research Sadie and I were going to do. I wondered why this seemed to upset her. When Lola left the shop, I turned to Sadie. "Come to think of it, I never did any research on Lola when she came to town. She seemed so pathetic as she mourned the death of her friend, Jana, and seemed so alone that I just accepted her at face value. I figured, if Jana trusted Lola, she must be okay. I had a great deal of respect for the costume designer and was sorry to hear of her death. You don't suppose Lola has anything to hide, do you? She seems so open and transparent, but then again, she is quite a good actress. I think this whole investigation is getting to me. I seem to be suspecting everyone."

"Robin, we're all getting a bit paranoid, I think,"

said Sadie. "I even find myself looking over my shoulder wherever I go. There is still a murderer at large, and we're nowhere closer to determining who it is. At least, in our village, ISIS was a known evil. Now we're facing an unknown evil. That's scary."

"Don't worry, Sadie," I said. "The boys are looking out for you. We all have your back."

"I must admit, it's great to have such wonderful friends. Thank you, Robin," Sadie said, wiping away a tear.

I am getting worried about Sadie. I hope she's as strong as she pretends to be.

Chapter 17

Unknown Lola

Lola was in full panic mode when she heard about our research. *What if Robin and Sadie unearth my past while researching that of Tyler and Fergusson? If Robin and Sadie find out that I lied to them when I came to Pittman, they'll never trust me again. What should I do?*

Lola grew up in Chicago, but her family went to Lennon, not far from Pittman, each summer where her parents performed in a bluegrass band as an opening act at Tanglewood. Her dad took her to many outdoor performances during the summer theater season in the Berkshires. Seeing the plays and musical performances instilled in her a love of the theater.

For as long as she could remember, Lola had always wanted to be an actress. When she was five, and her brothers refused to let her play soccer with the big kids, Lola devised a devious way to get her father to intercede.

"Daddy, Milo and Reese won't let me play with them. I can kick the ball far. Just watch." Little Lola kicked her legs high and danced all around, while singing at the top of her voice, "I am the kicking soccer girl, soccer girl, soccer girl. I can kick higher than anyone, anyone, anyone." She kept on like this until her dad had had quite enough.

"Lola, stop right this minute," he yelled. "Go and play soccer and get some of that energy out of you. Tell the boys that I said so."

Lola was excited that she had found a new way to get what she wanted using her acting.

When Lola was six, another clever acting performance took place whenever she wanted something special. Lola would wait until her mom was out of the room, then she would crawl up on her dad's lap, lean her head on his shoulder, and start to sob. Then she would hiccup. Sob, hiccup, sob, hiccup. "*Who can resist a performance like this*," thought devious Lola. Inevitably, Lola got whatever she wanted from her dad if her mom didn't know about it.

Lola's acting abilities improved with age, as did her ability to manipulate and deceive others. Unfortunately, her mom never appreciated Lola's prowess and hated that her father gave her so much attention. She resented her daughter and heaped abuse on Lola for most of her childhood.

Lola's brothers looked upon her as the annoying bother that she was, and the only one who seemed to care for Lola was her crude father, a wannabe guitar superstar who had played in a band since he was in high school. He died from drug and alcohol abuse when Lola was a teen. She always felt her dad had abandoned her and just couldn't forgive him for loving drugs and alcohol more than her.

After her father's untimely death, her mom still brought them each summer to the Berkshires, but then she would take off on tour with the same band her dad played in, leaving Lola with her older brothers most of the time.

Lola spent very little time at home and threw herself into the Berkshire summer theater scene. At fourteen, she got a job ironing clothes in the costume department at the Shakespeare complex in Stockbridge where she became fast friends with a lovely lady, Jana, who was in her seventies and became a surrogate mother to love-starved Lola. At fifteen, Lola became a guide at the complex. She was responsible for making sure the children in various groups enjoyed themselves. She would grab a costume from the hundreds in the closet and pretend to be a sad ghost who needed protection.

"I am so sad," she would say. "Please help me find a home. Please hug me." The kids loved the sad ghost and ran up to her for a group hug.

Throughout her teen years, Lola saved all her money to pay for acting camps and learned to emote with the best. Audiences were in awe of her beautiful smile and ability to bring her characters to life. Little did they know that her beautiful smile hid the sorrows of a lonely girl who felt abandoned.

The one thing that Lola avoided was the drug scene. Because of her father's addiction, she blamed drugs, and her mother, for ruining her life. Adamant, when her friends tried to persuade her to just chill out and try a drug, everyone learned not to even mention drugs to Lola because her freak-out scene would not be pretty. Many times, Jana consoled sobbing Lola.

In one skit, the summer of her junior year in Stockbridge, Lola acted in a play where she had the role of three characters: an old lady down on her luck, a glamorous model, and a rowdy cheerleader. She had the audience laughing out loud at the scenes where her cheerleader called out the silliest cheers, and the glamorous model tripped going down the runway.

This acclaim from audiences led to Lola's plan to escape from her abusive mother. She did her community service project her senior year at the Chicago high school by conducting acting workshops for elementary school kids. That summer at Tanglewood, she volunteered at the kids' day and had the kids blowing instruments, constructing drums from boxes, and then parading around the grounds. Kids and parents loved her.

While acting in her first television role in Hollywood, CA, Lola got a frantic phone call from a director at the Shakespeare Playhouse. Jana was very ill and kept asking for Lola. Dropping everything, Lola drove cross-country to Stockbridge as fast as possible. Unfortunately, Jana died before she arrived.

For days, Lola cried and seemed to be paralyzed. She just couldn't function.

That's when I took pity and approached her after the funeral. "Lola, I know how close you were to Jana. I am so sorry for your loss. Jana will be a loss for all of us. Why don't you come to my house? Several friends will be over to support one another, have dinner, and talk about our times with Jana. I would love it if you were to join us."

"I don't know what I am going to do now. I don't want to go back to LA and look for work, and I can't return to Chicago. I just need some time to figure out what to do. Jana always counseled me when I had to make major decisions. I miss her so much," sobbed Lola.

I decided to help this despondent girl. It felt like payback since so many people helped me when I lost my husband, John. When I offered her a job at my bookstore, she was thrilled that she could live in Pittman and remain a part of the summer stock theater scene. My kindness led to a life change for Lola. Now she would do anything for me, even if it meant dealing with the devious Mr. Fergusson and annoying Tyler. She would use her acting abilities to take those men down.

Chapter 18

Intrigue at the Library

Saturday morning, Sadie and I met for breakfast muffins before the library opened to plot out our research plan.

"Sadie, you take Tyler and Fergusson. I'll take Lola and Billy. Let's dig into their pasts. Maybe we should also examine Sam's background and his treatment of Mike before Sam went to jail. Was he a good father? What happened to his wife, etc.? I also want to know more about Sheriff Houtman's past. Why did he leave Boston and come to a small place like Pittman? He hasn't really revealed much about himself since he came here."

I knew Sadie wanted to dig into Sheriff Houtman's past, but I was afraid she was too sweet on him, and if she found anything shady, she might suppress it.

When we got to the library, we spotted Tyler huddled with Mike's dad, Sam, in the computer section.

"What do you think they're up to? Both men keep whispering then looking to see if anyone overheard them." Sadie and I ducked behind a bookcase hidden from their sight. "This can't be good. Did you hear anything? Can you read lips by any chance?" I whispered to Sadie.

"I did hear Billy's name, and then Tyler said

something about a whole lot of money," said Sadie. "I'm worried about Billy. I'm almost sure it was Tyler who was lurking outside my house the other night when Billy stayed over. Billy thought he also saw Tyler just standing across the street. After about an hour, he moved on. Do you think he was spying on Billy or me? I don't like that man. What could they be plotting against the boy? He looks to be dirt poor, so how can they plan to get money from him? Do you think they're going to make him sell Tyler's drugs?" Sadie asked, puzzled.

"Maybe you've hit on their plan, but why Billy? You would think if Sam were involved, he would want his own son to get a piece of the action," I answered.

"Maybe Sam is protecting Mike, or maybe Sam is afraid if Mike got caught, the police might track the crime back to him," said Sadie.

"Uh oh, watch out. Here they come. Act natural so they don't suspect we're spying on them. "I know Sam is an alcoholic. He was in rehab while in prison, but I don't think he stuck with the program. Asher hinted that Sam was drunk the other night when he and Mike went bowling. He also said Mike stayed away from his dad when he was in a drunken state. Mike confided in Asher that Sam could be a very mean drunk and often got in trouble for fighting. That's part of why he ended up in jail. Sam can't hold his liquor. My guess is that he is then abusive to Mike. I'm not sure how Tyler holds his liquor, but I wonder why those two are hanging out together?"

As Tyler and Sam rose to go, they spotted us. I nodded to the two men and said innocently, "Greetings, gentlemen. You look so intense huddled at that table. I hope your day improves."

"Mind your own business, George. And you, Ms. Foreigner, I am getting angry seeing you stalking me," shouted Tyler. "I've a good mind to report you both to Sheriff Houtman and maybe get a restraining order."

Sadie rolled her eyes. "You go right ahead and get a restraining order. That would mean that I'm rid of you since you couldn't be near me either. Go for it. I dare you, you prejudiced dope."

I had to restrain Sadie, and Sam held Tyler back from rushing at Sadie.

"Let's just go have that drink. These nosy people will keep out of our business if they know what is good for them," said Sam as he led Tyler out the door toward Ten Pins.

Chapter 19

Mike's Dad and Mom

About one o'clock on Saturday, Mike entered Ten Pins Bowling Alley, hoping to slip past his dad and make some lunch since the refrigerator was bare at their apartment.

Sam yelled, "It's about time you decided to grace us with your presence! You're quite willing to help Ms. George at the bookstore with anything she needs, but do you ever lift a finger to help your own dad? Get in here and get to work, you lazy excuse for a son."

Mike bit his tongue to keep from yelling back. He knew from experience that if he smarted off, Sam would not hesitate to haul off and smack him. With Tyler as an audience, Mike knew he needed to make himself scarce. It was evident Sam was drinking again. He promised his parole officer and Mike that 'never again' would he touch a drop of liquor. "Yeah, right," thought Mike, "just like you promised Mom."

As Mike shuffled over to get the broom to spruce up the bar area, a memory of his mom flashed into his mind:

Mike's mom, Maria, was a beautiful lady. She came to this country on a student visa from Mexico. Maria met his dad at Boston College, her sophomore year. She was a talented math student and hoped to get a scholarship to graduate school and study law. Maria fell in love with Sam, and they were married her junior year. She dropped out of school when she was in her ninth month of pregnancy and never went back.

Things were going well for the family until Mike was about three.

Sam got a job as a manager at a shipping warehouse down by the port for a large distribution company. His power over others changed him. He thoroughly enjoyed bossing others around, and this power poisoned his family relationships.

On Friday nights, Sam told Maria that he needed to go to the local bar to hang out with his people. At first, Sam seemed to just need to socialize with his workers, so Maria gave in and let him go. Next, Sam told Maria that he needed to take clients out to dinner occasionally. Again, Maria accepted Sam's word. After all, he was making the money while she was staying home with Mike. Maria did some lovely embroidery that she sold to make extra income, and she did the accounting for several small businesses in the area. She kept that extra money from Sam just to give her a little insurance policy in case something happened to Sam.

The client dinners increased from occasionally to several times a week. Sam often came home drunk and in a belligerent mood. Finally, Maria had had it and put her foot down.

"Sam, you're a husband and a father," she said. "It's about time you quit carousing like a teenager and tend to your responsibilities."

That's when the beatings began. Mike learned by age four to hide whenever his dad got home past dinner time. Mike would grab his stuffed lion and crawl behind his dresser to listen to the noise. He would make his lion roar at his dad and often imagined his lion eating his dad. Mike would cry silently because he knew his dad was hurting his mom.

When Maria threatened to leave him, Sam would tell her he would report her to immigration because she had overstayed her student visa. Maria could lose Mike, so she cowered and took the beatings, refusing to fight back.

One night, when Mike was six, Sam beat Maria so badly that she lay bleeding on the floor when Sam left. Mike couldn't wake her up so he went next door to Mrs. Reilly and banged on the door. Sobbing, Mike told Mrs. Reilly what happened, and she called the paramedics. Maria ended up in the hospital, and they put Mike in foster care. He kept hoping his mother would come for him, but his foster parents explained that after Maria recovered, she was sent back to Mexico.

Mike cried himself to sleep each night and willed his lion to eat his dad. Meanwhile, Sam kept up his raucous ways, lost his job, and was caught stealing money from a local gas station where he also beat up the clerk. Mike's dad was taken to jail, tried, and sentenced to three years in prison.

Mike's foster parents explained all this to the quiet six-year-old. Mike smiled and said, "Yes, my lion ate my dad. Now, I don't have to see him again."

This was true until Mike turned nine, and Sam was released from prison. Sam tracked down Mike and convinced Social Services that he had reformed and wanted to make this all up to his son. The social worker believed him, and Mike went to live with an abusive dad who tried to reform, but couldn't quite stay on the straight and narrow, especially while drunk.

Mike snapped out of his trip down his haunting memory lane, finished cleaning up the bar, and slipped out the back door while Sam and Tyler were laughing about some scheme they were cooking up.

Thank goodness for Mike's friendship with Asher. Mike was able to crawl out of his silence and mask all his troubles with a humorous and engaging manner, though there were times like now when Mike wished he could summon his childhood friend and scream, "Lion, eat him."

Chapter 20

Sweet Indulgences

After leaving the library, Sadie and I returned to Sweet Indulgences. We needed a cup of her strong coffee and some cinnamon coffee cake to digest all we had found out in our research. Just as we sat, Sheriff Houtman came into the shop.

"Ladies." He smirked as he took a chair and joined us.

Widower or not, he can't just expect us to want his company socially. If he were a gentleman, he would ask if we would like him to join us.

Sadie, of course, smiled a friendly welcome and immediately fetched him some cinnamon coffee cake.

"Mmmm, thanks, Sadie. I just wanted to know what I should bring to the barbeque tonight," he said. "It sure was nice of you to invite me."

"Well, the Saturday barbeque has become a weekly tradition since Sadie moved here three years ago, right after John died." I hated that tears sprung to my eyes at the mention of John and was embarrassed that Sheriff Houtman saw this weak side of me. "Just bring anything you want. We like to be surprised," I said hastily to cover my embarrassment.

I quickly switched to interrogation mode. "What have you found out about the break-ins? What about the murder victim? Do you know who he is? Was anything taken from the Pharmacy or Joker's Den?"

"No, we don't think anything was taken," Houtman replied. "We're checking local ex-cons in the area, and we're running some fingerprints. Though the vandalism could be the work of teenage hooligans or vagrants," he said, meaning Billy, "I doubt they would have committed murder or been responsible for any vandalism. Oh well, nothing so far. We're putting a picture of the murder victim in the Sunday paper. Hopefully, someone will recognize him and give us a name. Do I need to warn you and Sadie again to leave the detecting to the professionals and tend to your own businesses?" he said as he gave me a reproachful look. "You two are always trying to solve mysteries that are really none of your business."

"For your information," I raged at the snarky sheriff, "this *is* our business when you say your chief suspects are teenagers, meaning my son, Asher, and his friends, and that poor boy Billy. If you can't find other suspects, then you leave us no choice but to find the real culprits."

This seemed like the perfect opportunity to tell him what we found out about Tyler and Sam's sinister plot, whatever it is, and get him to investigate, but just as I started, a call came in from his dispatcher, and he had to leave abruptly. With a friendly smile and a wink at Sadie, he said, "Thanks. The coffee cake was delicious. You're a great cook, Sadie."

"Oh, Sadie, that man makes me so mad. We've done nothing but help him with investigations in the past, and he fails to appreciate any suggestions we make. I know you are sweet on him, but he makes me so angry sometimes."

Sadie looked sheepishly at me. "Robin, give him a chance. You both are just bull-headed. That's why you clash so. He really does have a soft, sweet side under all that bluster, and he loves my cooking."

"Yeah, right. A soft, sweet side? I don't think so, and just how do you know about his sweet side?" I blurted out.

Sadie blushed. I turned and slammed the door of Sweet Indulgences as I left. Sadie and I never argued, but that man pushes all my wrong buttons.

Fuming as I drove home, I began to think about Sheriff Houtman. *What do I really know about him personally except that his wife died before he came to Pittman? What kind of sheriff was he in Boston? Why did he leave? Did he leave because of some wrongdoing? You would think he would want to stay in the town where he shared history with his deceased wife. Also, what was his history with his wife? Were they happily married? Why weren't there any children, or were there? How did his wife die? Were there any mysterious circumstances?*

I decided I would discuss these questions at the first opportunity with Sadie and Lola. In the meantime, I intended to do more research on the irritating sheriff. Since Houtman seems a bit sweet on Sadie, maybe she can pry some answers out of him. This barbeque could prove revealing.

When I got home, I spent an hour on the computer trying to unearth some info on Sheriff Houtman's prior life.

Chapter 21

Research

As I was researching Sheriff Houtman's past, I came across an article in the *Boston Globe*.

"Whoa!" I said after about an hour of reading. I immediately called Sadie. "Listen to this article, Sadie, in the *Boston Globe* about Sheriff Houtman." I read the article to her.

Accidental Death?

Why is Sheriff Houtman not pressing charges against the teenager whose Range Rover plowed into his wife? Tom Ply was setting off on his first solo drive since he got his driver's license. Ashe drove down the block, he took the curve at a moderate speed, but Tom lost control. When his Range Rover swerved, he crashed into Mrs. Adele Houtman outside her house as she was about to bring in their trash can. The force of the car caused Mrs. Houtman to fall backward and hit her head on the concrete. A neighbor witnessed the crash and called 911, Sheriff Mark Houtman, and Tom's mother rushed to the crash scene. The EMT told Sheriff Houtman the sad news that Mrs. Houtman was unresponsive, and there was no pulse.

I hurriedly searched the paper for a follow-up article and found one several days later.

Sheriff Refuses to Press Charges

Sheriff Mark Houtman, whose wife was killed by a newly licensed teenage driver, has refused to press a charge of reckless homicide against Tom Ply. Ply's family expressed their relief and sorrow and thanked Sheriff Houtman for his understanding.

I called Sadie again and relayed this new finding.

"Robin, why do you think he refused to press charges? Do you think Mark Houtman hates Billy because a teenager killed his wife?"

"I don't know what to think, Sadie. It's strange the articles say nothing about Mrs. Houtman. Usually, when a tragedy like this happens, the newspaper unearths all the facts about the victim, the husband, the driver, and the neighbors. Someone has the power to hush things up. I wonder why?"

"Do we know yet why the sheriff left his post in Boston?" asked Sadie.

"No, but I'm certainly going to ask him about it."

My next phone call was to the sheriff. "I need to see you about some important information I uncovered. I'm headed over to my bookstore now to relieve Lola. Can you meet me there at about five?"

Chapter 22

Mary Beth and Shine

Sadie was joining me for the meeting with the sheriff. Promptly at five, Sheriff Houtman entered my bookstore. When I confronted him about the newspaper articles, he closed his eyes and lowered his head.

"I guess I owe you two snoops an explanation," he said. "I left Boston because of a personal tragedy, not because of incompetence on the job. My supervisor begged me to stay, but I just needed to get away."

He looked at us with sad eyes and continued, "After my wife died, my girlfriend throughout high school in Boston, Mary Beth Ply, a beautiful cheerleader who had lived next door to me, contacted me to express her sympathy.

"When I returned to Boston after four years, Mary Beth had already returned. She'd quit college three months from graduation. When I sat on her porch and begged her to tell me why she left college, she began to cry. I had never seen her cry. I had asked what was so bad that she couldn't tell me?" He paused. "We were best friends forever. Whatever was wrong, she knew I could handle it.

"After several drinks, Mary Beth poured out her heart to me that night. Brian Mayther had gotten her drunk one night and took her to a sleazy hotel and raped her. When she woke the next morning, she was in a strange bed in a dirty hotel room and naked. No Brian. Mary Beth was so ashamed and angry, she got dressed and slunk home. She promised herself that she would get back at that scumbag, Brian.

"Two months later, she realized she was pregnant. She went to a doctor to confirm it, and being a very religious person, she couldn't have an abortion. All she knew was that she needed help to start a new life far away from Brian, who was in most of her classes. That's when she dropped out of school, so close to graduation.

"She didn't know how to tell her parents about the baby. With the help of a few friends, she finally faced her parents, who were astonished but happy about the prospect of having a grandchild, so they forgave her. When Shine was born, Mary Beth was delighted. She and her parents fussed over this beautiful baby girl. Mary Beth got a job at the library and lived peacefully in our old Boston neighborhood for the next ten years.

"Mary Beth and I talked about the hit and run, and the tragedy of a life that ended too soon. I told her how devastated I was about Adele's death and how empty I felt. Mary Beth broke down, sobbed, and collapsed into my arms. 'I need your help. It was my brother who hit Adelle. Please have mercy and don't prosecute him. Do you remember what a cute little kid Tommy was, particularly when he would sneak up on us when we were talking on my porch? He's so special to me. Please forgive him for getting drunk and ruining your life. I beg you not to ruin his life. Do it for me.'

"Holidays were spent with Mary Beth's family, and Adele and I always felt their friendship. Her brother

Tommy looked up to me, and when he thought I wasn't looking, he would stand tall and mimic my walking. We would laugh heartily at his antics. I had to help her. I didn't press charges against Tommy. I couldn't do that to his family, but the immature jerk that I was, I couldn't face Mary Beth without seeing Adele's face in my thoughts, so I fled to this small town to start over again. I feel so guilty, but it was an unfortunate accident that has plagued me."

Sadie and I were stunned. We didn't know what to say. Here we were suspecting evil deeds, and all the while the sheriff was a grieving husband. "Well," I finally said, "I guess we have to cross you off our suspect list."

Sadie turned to Sheriff Houtman and patted his arm. "I am so sorry," she said, and then quickly changed the subject.

We haven't found much so far in our investigations, but we'll keep digging. Have you found anything on Tyler or Fergusson yet? You know, it seems confusing to us. In our research, we found several references to Fergusson, but none are tied to any real estate firms. Tyler is such a common name that I am finding him hard to trace also since we don't know many details of his life. Since we don't know much about Lola before she came to Pittman, we also are searching her background, but nothing so far."

Back in the reality of the moment, the sheriff said, "Ladies, leave the searching to the police. You are in way over your heads. Right now, Billy is our best suspect whether you like it or not."

The sheriff left, looking shaken by the confession about his time in Boston.

Chapter 23

The Barbeque

When I pulled into my driveway, I heard loud laughter from the backyard. They all were playing a game of Charades. Mike was using the patio as a stage as he impersonated Mopey Tyler. "I hate Robin George. I hate Sadie. I hate that inept sheriff. I'm so glad everyone loves me, the king of Farley Square."Mike was prancing around like a circus pony as he talked in an exaggerated, high, whiny voice. "Who am I?" he said.

Everyone yelled, "Mopey Tyler."

"Let me do one; let me do one," Lola demanded. She stepped onto the patio stage and thought for a minute. "Oh, Mrs. Rich, of course I can find you a wonderful house in Pittman. Let me first just evict the people who are living there." Then she danced in a loop around the group singing, "Oh, when I am a rich man, la, la, la, la, la."

Everyone giggled and shouted, "Fergusson, the real estate King."

I was glad to see that the barbeque had begun in such a hilarious tone, but being the mother that I am, I couldn't condone making fun of others, even if it was true. I quickly ended the game by giving jobs to everyone. Mike and Asher were going to grill the hamburgers on our two-layered grill. Houtman and Billy, when they got here, would help them, and Lola could set up the long folding table with all the delicious goodies they each brought. We had a feast of appetizers: hummus and pita bread, shrimp and cocktail sauce, hot pretzels and cheese dip, and salami and cream cheese rollups. The hungry guests dragged lawn chairs, cardtable chairs, and more folding tables from the garage. Then those who weren't cooking sat down to relax.

As we eased into the lawn chairs with plates of appetizers, Sheriff Houtman came around the side of the house and into our backyard, not looking very happy. "Where's Billy?" he snapped at Asher and Mike.

Spatula in hand, Asher said, "He was supposed to be here an hour ago. He's our assistant chef. We don't know why he isn't here. Billy isn't usually late to any event, especially if it involves food. If anything, he's usually early. Is there a problem?"

"The problem is Billy just became our number one suspect in the band member's murder. We've identified the victim in the alley as Bobby Jo Love, a guitar player in the Lovey Dove Bluegrass Band. We know from the school band members that Billy is a fan of Bluegrass music. An eyewitness came forward who saw Billy go into Tyler's store right about the time of the robbery. He may very well have committed the robbery and vandalism."

"Who's the witness?" several people said at once.

"Myrna Marshall, a secretary, who just heard that we wanted eyewitnesses to come forward," said Houtman.

Lola jumped in. "Myrna Marshall, why she's the secretary that Fergusson just fired at Welcome Realty. While I was working there part-time, she was telling me she had done some snooping and found out that Fergusson planned to put up a condo complex complete with housing units and high-end retail stores. Fergusson walked in during our conversation, but Myrna didn't think he overheard her accuse him. The next day though, Fergusson called Myrna into his office and accused her of stealing from petty cash. Being the upright churchgoer that she is, the accusation outraged her, and she denied it vehemently. Nevertheless, Fergusson fired her on the spot with no severance pay, told her to clean out her desk and leave immediately. If looks could kill, Myrna would have killed Fergusson right then. She needed that job. She lives alone, supports herself, and has some high medical bills.

"Myrna cleaned out her desk, retaliating by wreaking havoc, throwing anything that wasn't hers all over the floor. She also went into the breakroom and took all the coffee grounds and tossed them all over the rug. Then she opened the copy paper box and scattered the papers everywhere. After that rampage, Myrna calmed down, picked up her belongings, marched to Fergusson's door to his office, and shouted, "You will regret this, Fergusson. I promise you will pay for this injustice. Good luck finding anyone to work for you. You are a jerk."

"And what happened after that?" I asked.

"Myrna is probably accusing Billy so she can throw the blame off herself. She probably trashed Klette's Pharmacy and The Joker's Den because she wanted to get back at Fergusson for firing her. By

Myrna attacking his friends' stores, Fergusson would get nervous that this vandalism would discourage investors." Lola turned to Houtman. "Sheriff, you should be worried right now that she is planning to take down Fergusson and anyone associated with him."

"I'm sure Myrna is mad and justifiably so," Sadie said. "I can see her vandalizing the stores, but she is a very religious person. She wouldn't murder a young man."

Everyone looked at Houtman to see how he took this news of Myrna's rampage. He appeared deep in thought about what Lola said, but then questioned us all. "If Myrna is the guilty party, then where is Billy? Why isn't he here? Does Billy know that Myrna witnessed him going into The Joker's Den right before the robbery so he ran off?"

This was getting ridiculous. I told the sheriff, "I employed Myrna part-time right after she left Welcome Realty. She is a lovely woman and has done a great job in my bookstore."

"Then why would she lie about seeing Billy and try to blame him for the vandalism?" Frustrated, Asher ran his hand through his hair and looked at me for reassurance.

"Let's get to the bottom of this. Asher. Call Billy's cell phone. See where he is and tell him to get right over here to clear up this mess. Lola, since you know Fergusson, call him and ask if he has spoken to Myrna since she left his employment," I said in a firm voice.

Sheriff Houtman just stared at me. "Robin, I'm still in charge of this investigation. Don't forget that."

Because of this distraction with Myrna and Billy, I couldn't meet with the others to go over those who had motives, and I couldn't share any of our research with Sheriff Houtman. That would just have to wait until later.

What Sheriff Houtman and all the rest of us didn't know about was the subject of a discussion between Fergusson, Tyler, and Sam. Though Sadie and I had seen Fergusson and Tyler at the library, we had no idea of the diabolical scheme they were devising.

Chapter 24

The Plot Thickens

Early last week, when Fergusson saw Billy asleep on the floor of my bookstore, Fergusson called Billy "Robin's tramp". Then Fergusson got curious. Robin had mentioned Billy's strange behavior at Story Time when Lola was reading *Fire, the Hiccupping Dragon*. Piecing together bits of information, Fergusson figured out that Billy's odd behavior must have something to do with that children's book. Fergusson was suspicious of Billy, so he decided to follow the money. Since researching was one of Fergusson's strengths, he tracked down the dragon book and the author's name, Dehlia Woods.

At first, Fergusson just wanted to cause Robin trouble for harboring a runaway so he could close down her bookstore and buy the property to expand his influence on Farley Square. But when Fergusson researched Billy's background and the book, he discovered Dehlia Woods was a prolific author who made a fortune in royalties from her books, the film rights for those books, and novelty items related to the books. Dollar signs flashed in his eyes as he searched.

Fergusson found a newspaper article about Dehlia Woods' legacy and discovered that when she died last year, she left the rights to all her books in print and out of print, as well as all the movie rights and profits from the novelty items to her nephew, but her lawyers had been unable to locate the nephew. The lawyers tracked down Aunt Dehlia's parents, but the Woods, Billy's possible grandparents, were deceased. A neighbor told the lawyers that the Woods had a grandson, who disappeared right after the funeral. The description in the paper was vague, but he would be the same age as Billy, and the description of his wild hair fit Billy. *Could her nephew be Billy*?

Fergusson researched the possibility that Billy had this huge inheritance, and that inheritance was the subject of Fergusson and Tyler's secretive discussion at Ten Pins Bowling Alley. Fergusson said to Tyler, "Dehlia Woods was worth millions. The money from the sales of that book and the sales of the stuffed animals and other paraphernalia associated with that crazy dragon brought her scads of money over the years. Then that kids' book was made into a movie that was a huge success at the box office. She wrote five more books, each more successful than the others, and each film more lucrative than the last. If Billy is her nephew, he inherits millions."

"Wow," said Tyler. "Do you think we can cash in on this? Any idea how?"

Greedy Tyler was intrigued when Fergusson told him about the inheritance. If there's one thing Tyler and Fergusson had in common, it was their love of money. If they could get their hands on Aunt Dehlia's millions, they could leave the country and set up shop somewhere beautiful and warm. No more snow. No more Massachusetts.

"We need help with this plot," Fergusson said.

"It's too risky to do on our own," continued Fergusson. "Let's involve Sam. If anything goes wrong, we'll have a scapegoat."

Later that day, Fergusson approached the bar to get some nachos and asked Sam to join him and Tyler at their table. Sam was anxious to hear what the two men had to say and what they had been so animatedly discussing, so he grabbed the nachos and sauce and headed to their table.

Sam pulled up a chair to join the two men, and Fergusson began. "We have a proposition for you that could make you a lot of money."

Tyler sat up and paid attention this time as Fergusson laid out the plan.

Fergusson revealed the devious kidnapping plan he and Tyler had concocted. "Sam, we need your help. You're crucial to this plan because Billy probably has no idea who you are."

Little did either of them know Billy was a friend of Mike's and certainly knew him, but Sam kept that knowledge to himself.

Fergusson then spelled out the steps in the kidnapping plan. "Sam, you'll disguise yourself as a homeless tramp and then kidnap Billy, the kid who crashed into Robin's bookstore. Here's a picture of him from a newspaper article I found right after the vandalism in town. When you snatch him, you'll pull a burlap sack over his head and take him in a borrowed truck to a warehouse that I own up near Lake Onota. When you get inside the warehouse, tie him up, then go outside the warehouse, and stand guard. Tyler and I will arrive afterward and question the kid."

Sam was smart enough to figure out that the two

men wanted him on board as a scapegoat if anything went wrong, but Sam needed the money offered by Fergusson. He also saw a way to retaliate against Tyler by turning the tables and implicating Tyler, not himself, in the scheme. Sam hated Tyler because his smutty business was bringing down the standards of the shops on Farley Square, and Sam was losing money.

Some of his customers didn't want to bring their kids to a bowling alley next to a sex shop, and Sam didn't like the temptation for Mike and the teens to try his drugs. Plus, Sam suspected that Tyler, with his buddy Fergusson, would jump right in and buy Ten Pins Bowling Alley if Sam defaulted on his loan or was sent to jail for kidnapping. Sam desperately needed to get rid of The Joker's Den.

Sam didn't know much about Billy except that Mike and he were in the band together, and according to Tyler, Billy was just some tramp who crashed in town at the local children's bookstore. He saw no harm in working with Tyler and Fergusson on their scheme to kidnap Billy and reap a large cash reward.

Once Sam took Billy to the warehouse, stood guard, then turned him over to Fergusson, his part in the kidnapping would be over. He would be richer and home free. No one would trace Sam back to Fergusson. His employee, Frank, at the bowling alley would swear Sam was working at Ten Pins all afternoon. They always vouched for each other, and Frank could be trusted to have his back. Frank had been Sam's bunkmate while in prison. Ex-cons supported each other. Grateful for a second chance and having no family of his own except a long-lost son, Frank would do anything for Sam and considered him not only a friend but family.

All these thoughts went through Sam's head as he poured drinks for Tyler, Fergusson, and himself. Yes, kidnapping Billy seemed like an excellent idea.

Tyler and Fergusson hoped the kidnapping plot would shake Billy to the point he'd sign over all royalties accrued so far from books and movies to an unnamed person. Tyler will take the signed document to Fergusson at his realty office, and Fergusson will give the guardianship document to a trusted lawyer friend of his to fill out the necessary legal forms so they will have power of attorney over Billy's money. Then Fergusson will transfer the funds.

"We'll threaten Robin, Sadie, and anyone else Billy knows until he signs the paperwork." Fergusson looked at the two of them with a sinister gleam in his eyes. "If necessary, we'll threaten to kill him if he dares reveal the truth to anyone."

Fergusson continued outlining the plan. "I'll meet with my lawyer and have papers drawn up to make Tyler and me Billy's legal guardians should Billy be found. At that point, Tyler and I will present the document to the others as a *fait accompli* saying Tyler and I only had Billy's interests at heart since Billy has no expertise in handling large sums of money. If Billy isn't found, then we could come forward after Billy's death or disappearance with the guardianship papers. Legally, then Tyler and I would inherit all of Aunt Dehlia's wealth.

Unbeknownst to Tyler, Fergusson had another paper drawn up that would transfer all of Tyler's money to himself. He planned to slip that paper into the stack of papers that Tyler and Billy would sign, and Tyler will be none the wiser.

Chapter 25

Meeting at the Lawyer's Office

Mr. Wright of the firm Wright and Peterson said, "I would like to meet Billy in person, but if, as you say, he has no interest in the money from the book rights or inheritance, you will need to bring me an affidavit that states he denounces the inheritance and turns it over entirely to you or Tyler, or both of you since you say that's Billy's plan."

"Yes, that's exactly what he said when we told him about his Aunt Dehlia's legacy. He's a kid with no experience with large sums of money. We've cared for Billy since he first appeared in Pittman many months ago and want to be sure he's not making any mistakes with this inheritance. Billy knows I'm a whiz with finances and trusts me to do what is best for him investment-wise. The only book he wants the rights to is *Fire, the Hiccupping Dragon* because of his emotional attachment to it," said Fergusson. "We need to establish this guardianship soon because we're afraid that others are trying to bilk Billy out of his inheritance."

Tyler thought it was a brilliant stroke of genius to throw in the part about the book. This made Fergusson's story much more believable and removed all concerns that he might be taking advantage of a kid.

Mr. Wright said, "I'll draw up a contract that gives
the profits from the book to Billy and one that gives
you both joint guardianship of all other profits, but the
profits must be used to help support Billy. You will be
made financial guardians of his estate. I'll need,
however, to talk to Billy, or if he's as shy and
disinterested as you say, he'll need to write me a letter
assigning the managing of his estate to you."

As they left the lawyer's office, Fergusson and
Tyler congratulated themselves on the tale they
concocted about Billy being so shy with strangers that
he would break out in hives when he had to talk to a
strange man. They told the lawyer that this stemmed
from the isolated life Billy had lived on his grandpa's
dairy farm. Something bad must have happened to scare
him about meeting male strangers. He seemed okay
with women like Ms. George and kids his own age, like
Asher, but he sure was a mess when he had to deal with
men.

When Mr. Wright heard this story, he agreed to
honor a written permission document signed by Billy
when they brought it back to his office.

Chapter 26

Implementation of the Kidnap Plan

Fergusson, Tyler, and Sam meant to implement this elaborate kidnapping plan while Robin's group was at the barbeque on Saturday. They assumed a tramp like Billy certainly wouldn't be invited to the barbeque, and no one in the neighborhood would miss him. They agreed to snatch Billy at 5:30 p.m. Saturday. After getting the signed transfer of rights from Billy, Tyler will take the document to Fergusson. Both will then drop off the document at Fergusson's lawyer's house to make everything official. Then they would go back to town separately.

If Billy refused to sign, they would keep him prisoner until he agreed to sign away his inheritance. They needed to hold him until Tuesday to have time to pick up the documents from the lawyer and then meet with the bank manager to transfer funds. If someone found Billy after that, fine. If not, fine too. Tough luck, Billy. Fergusson and Tyler would be long gone before the sheriff figured anything out.

Sam realized Fergusson and Tyler had an escape plan. Did they think they could drop everything on him? He needed some time to think and make sure they didn't make him the scapegoat for Billy's kidnapping. After his felony, he had no desire to go back to prison.

He decided there were only two choices. One, he could somehow get rid of Tyler and convince Fergusson to take him on as a partner instead, or two, he could threaten Fergusson and Tyler with blackmail after the kidnapping. Sam's head hurt just thinking about these schemes, but he was desperate. His bowling alley was his link to the legitimate world of business. Prison had left deep scars on Sam and a deep sense of shame that he had been caught. Never again would he suffer such humiliation.

He went back to his office in Ten Pins to do some soul searching and sinister plotting. He needed to reveal everything to Frank. That way, if something happened to him, Frank would look out for Mike's interest. Since Tyler and Fergusson had an escape plan, Sam just wanted to make sure their plan didn't include getting rid of Sam after his part in the kidnapping.

"Frank," Sam called out, "take a break. I have something I need to share with you."

Chapter 27

The Botched Kidnapping

Fergusson sped up the timetable on their kidnapping plan and act alone. That way, he wouldn't have to split the money with Tyler, a man he secretly abhorred. He also didn't trust Tyler. Fergusson was having recurring nightmares in which Tyler grabbed him, pointed a gun to his head, and executed him. Then he imagined Tyler on a secluded island in the Caribbean, in a mansion surrounded by riches that belonged to Fergusson. He'd wake up in a sweat, terrified. He needed to put an end to Tyler, soon, so the Thursday before the barbeque, Fergusson took matters into his own hands.

Wearing a mask and sweats that were too big on him, Fergusson confronted Billy as he walked down a deserted alley on the way home that afternoon after band practice. Waving a gun, Fergusson grabbed Billy's collar and demanded he come with him quietly, or he would use the gun shoved into Billy's back.

"Okay, kid, we know about your inheritance from Aunt Dehlia. I'm taking you to a secret warehouse, and you're going to sign some legal papers giving up the rights to any inheritance. You'll do this willingly and quietly. If you make a fuss or refuse, this gun will determine your future. Move along," demanded

Fergusson in a deep, gravelly voice. "Don't try to escape, or I will shoot."

****

Terrified, he also had the sense Fergusson wouldn't kill him if he needed his signature to get the money he was talking about, so Billy struggled with the realtor and managed to wrench himself free. He then ran for his life. There was no way Fergusson would catch up to a strong sprinter like himself.

After escaping, Billy pondered what the kidnapper had said. *What inheritance was he talking about? How could Aunt Dehlia have left him money?* She wasn't rich as far as he knew. This whole thing seemed impossible. At first, Billy considered going to Sheriff Houtman, but would the sheriff believe him? Sheriff Houtman had shown he didn't think too highly of him and was suspicious because Billy's parents were nowhere to be found. The sheriff also believed Billy might be responsible for the death of the Bluegrass rocker in the alley.

No, I can't trust the sheriff.

He thought about his friends, Asher, and Mike, but if he told them, he knew they would involve Sadie and Ms. George. *That idea is also out.* Billy decided he needed to disappear until he figured out what was going on and who was threatening him. An armed man accosting him wasn't anything to play around with. He needed to get out of town, but how?

When he heard Mrs. Drew's rickety station wagon clattering down the road, Billy jumped up and waved at kindly Mrs. Drew. When she stopped, he explained there was an emergency and he needed to get to Lennon. "I was hitchhiking to Lennon when I saw you,

Mrs. Drew. Are you headed to Lennon to shop? I'd be grateful for a ride," said Billy.

Mrs. Drew had been nice enough to hire Billy for some odd jobs. She was a retired widow with no children in the area. She lived alone and was grateful to Billy for his help. "I appreciate your raking my leaves last week. I'll be glad to give you a lift. I'm headed to the library there to play party bridge with some friends. A group of us play bridge each week and catch up on the latest gossip from Pittman. Hop right in, Billy."

Billy hitched a ride with Mrs. Drew, figuring the kidnapper would not look for him in Lennon, the next town over. "Thanks, Mrs. Drew. Would you do me one more favor and not tell anyone that you gave me a lift? I don't want anyone to know about this emergency. It's personal."

"Well, of course, I won't tell anyone," said Mrs. Drew.

She headed to the library after she dropped Billy off on Main Street.

In one of the gift shops, Billy bought a cap to hide his wild hair and hopefully, keep anyone from recognizing him. Scared, Billy wandered the small town filled with quaint shops and aromatic restaurants.

I'm so hungry, but I don't dare stop to eat. I need to get somewhere safe where no one will find me. I need time to think."

He spotted a homeless shelter, Welcome House, on the edge of town. *That seems as safe a place as any.*

Billy went into Welcome House and told the social worker, who greeted him a sad tale. "My mother was on her way to pick me up from Pittman where I was visiting Ms. Aboud, her lifelong friend, and mom had an accident. She's in the hospital in Ohio until her broken leg can heal. I was going to hitchhike to Ohio to be with Mom, but then I decided she wouldn't be pleased with that idea.

"I made it as far as Lennon, but I need to rethink this crazy idea. Ohio is quite far, and who knows what type of character would give me a ride. May I stay here for a few days to sort everything out? I won't be a bother, and I certainly don't want to worry Ms. Aboud or my mom. Once I decide what to do, I'll be on my way."

Billy smiled broadly at the social worker, hoping to charm her, but the wise woman said, "What's the name of the hospital so I can let your mom know where you are?

Billy pretended to look in his pocket, then whirled his head up, looking distressed. "I had it on a piece of paper, but I must have lost it when I tripped walking down the highway."

"What is Ms. Aboud's phone number?" asked the now suspicious social worker.

Billy quickly made up a number, hoping to buy some time.

"I'm really tired and hungry. Do you think I could come in and lie down?" sulked Billy.

"Okay, but just until I contact your mom or Ms. Aboud. Get a sandwich from our cook then go to room 15 and lie down until dinner. I'll let you know when I hear from someone."

When Billy settled into the shelter, he pondered his options after the botched kidnapping. *Why would someone want to kill me? That masked man was scary. And what was this inheritance the stranger kept yelling about? How does he even know about my Aunt Dehlia?*

He smiled remembering all the fond memories of Aunt Dehlia, and the locket she gave him with her picture in it. It was a present for his sixth birthday. *'Billy, this locket will remind you that you are always loved.'*

Billy stopped shivering from fear and finally fell asleep on the cot in the warm shelter.

****

That night, Fergusson decided that even though he had hoped to deny Tyler any part of the inheritance, he needed to enlist Tyler's and Sam's help. He should have just waited and proceeded as planned. With the three of them, they could overpower Billy once they found him

Fergusson picked up the phone and dialed. "Tyler, we need to meet to discuss the kidnapping plan. Meet me by lane ten at Sam's Bowling Alley at 8:00 p.m. Something terrible has gone wrong with our plan, and bring Sam. We're going to need his muscle, so we'll have to include him."

Chapter 28

Kidnapping Plans Revisited

At Sam's Bowling Alley, Fergusson explained how he had tried to kidnap Billy on his own, hoping to protect Tyler and Sam from any blame. He apologized to them. "I just didn't want either of you to get in trouble if anything went wrong. I fully intended to share the money with you both because you helped produce the plan. I botched the kidnapping by not realizing how strong a threatened teenager can be. You should have seen Billy scratch and scream. Look at the red blotches on my arms. I'm going to need your help if we're to going to carry this off. I have a new approach that involves the three of us."

Tyler rose from the bench on lane ten and began pacing. After Fergusson laid out his new scheme, which involved all three of the men kidnapping Billy, Tyler proposed a clever plan of his own. "Billy doesn't know I associate with you, so he has no reason to mistrust me. Why don't we track him down, then I'll approach him and befriend him? After listening to his sad story about how someone tried to kidnap him, I can spring a trap and lure him to your warehouse building telling him that he needs to lay low for awhile, that he'll be safe there, and I'll try to find his abductor. After a day or two, Fergusson and I go to the warehouse, confront him about his inheritance from his aunt, and threaten him if he doesn't sign over his inheritance to us."

"There's a major problem with both of your plans," interrupted Sam. "If he signs over his inheritance, Billy will have Sheriff Houtman on your tail before you can get any of the money. How are you going to manage that?"

Fergusson already had a response to that. "We'll hold Billy until the money is transferred into our accounts. Then we'll wire the money to an offshore account. Only then will we release him. He can tell anyone he wants to about the abduction and coercion because we won't be in town. I'll open a new realty company somewhere on the Caribbean Island. I've started over before, but this time with plenty of money to do so. Tyler will do what he does by opening the Island Joker's Den. I'll purchase the plane tickets ahead of time. Sam, just tell me where you want to relocate."

"Wait a minute," sputtered Sam. "You never said anything about relocating. I can't leave the area. I'm still on parole and must stay in the country. Also, I just started to mend my relationship with Mike. I can't desert him again."

"That's okay. The only part you'll have in all this is the actual kidnapping, and you'll be heavily disguised. Billy will have no idea who you are. We can just deposit your share of the money in several discreet accounts of your choosing. No one will be the wiser. If questioned about the deposits, make up a story about a windfall in sales at the bowling alley or a deposit on a future event at the bowling alley, or make up a rich uncle who died and left you the money."

"You two better know what you're doing. I'm not

going to be left holding the bag." *Maybe I need to listen to my conscience rather than these two con men.*

"You worry too much," Fergusson said. "Okay, now that we're all in agreement, where do you suppose Billy went?"

"That's your department. You're the great researcher, and it's your fault he escaped. Find him," yelled Tyler.

Fergusson said, "Okay, okay, no need to get upset again. I'll find him. He can't have gone far."

Sam added, "Mike was talking about a barbeque at Asher's house. I'm sure Billy plans to attend."

Tyler and Fergusson were so surprised by Sam's comment, they both blurted out, "Are you saying that Billy is friends with Asher and Mike?

We were so sure that no one would miss him for quite awhile since he was a stranger in town."

"No, I think Billy has lived here for about three months. And yes, Billy knows Mike and Asher."

Tyler asked, "Does Billy have parents here in Pittman who will be concerned with his disappearance?"

"Not that I know of, but they must live here somewhere?"

Tyler turned to Fergusson. "So much for your great research. Now we're in a pickle."

"Wherever Billy is, he must be in walking or biking distance, or he hitched a ride somewhere close. If he hitched a ride, we should be able to track down the good Samaritan who would pick up a teenager as scruffy looking as Billy. I'll do a systematic search and get back to you as soon as I find him. When we do, we'll abscond him to the warehouse and have Billy send a text to his parents and Mike and Asher saying that he's with a friend at the Finger Lakes for a few days since it's spring break. Obviously, this kid is a free spirit, so his parents shouldn't be too suspicious of his frivolous absence for a few days. It's important that our threats of harm to him and his friends are convincing enough to scare him to do whatever we say," said Fergusson with confidence.

Fergusson spent most of Thursday night searching the computer and interviewing people in the small town. Gossip always abounds in Pittman, and someone surely saw Billy hitchhiking and being picked up by someone, if that was the case.

Friday morning, looking rumpled like he hadn't slept all night, Fergusson rushed into The Joker's Den yelling for Tyler.

"Hold on; I'm with a customer. Have some respect," shouted Tyler.

Fergusson roamed the shop fuming and rubbing his angry fingers through his balding hair. *What a pompous flop of a man. Why did I ever get mixed up with him?* He paced the shop, going up and down each aisle, taking deep breaths as he walked.

From the shelves in The Joker's Den, Fergusson picked up cups with photos of women in all types of compromising positions and calendars with sexy pictures of women or men. Take your choice. "Why would anyone buy any of this horrid stuff? What type of man would sell this smut? Tyler must have had a deprived childhood," Fergusson muttered.

When Tyler's customer completed his purchase and left, Tyler guided the anxious Fergusson to his back office. "Take it easy. Do you want everyone to know we're up to something? You must be discreet. No more scenes in front of my customers," hissed Tyler. "Now, did you find the sneaky kid?"

"Yeah, I found him. The widow Diane Drew was heading to Lennon for her monthly luncheon with her bridge biddies when she spotted Billy hitchhiking on Colt Road and picked him up.

"She took Billy to Lennon and thought she saw him head to the Welcome House homeless shelter, and of course, had to tell all her cronies of her kindness to a poor downtrodden boy. Luckily, one of those cronies spilled the beans to me." Fergusson rubbed his hands together. "Now that we know where Billy is, here's what we must do."

Fergusson called Sam to explain his part in the kidnapping and about the search for Billy in Lennon. "Sam, you can make up an excuse to have Mike call you if Billy shows up at the barbeque. You can say you're trying to reach Billy to offer him a job for a couple of weeks, and you need to talk to him."

"Just a minute. Just a cotton-picking minute. You conjured up the first plan that, need I remind you, failed colossally? This time we're doing it my way. If not, you're on your own," Tyler said as he angrily stabbed Fergusson in the chest with his finger. "No mention of this to Mike. He'll just get suspicious. Plus, we promised Sam only limited involvement in the scheme. If he calls Mike about Billy, he exposes himself to being accused of complicity when Billy disappears."

Biting his tongue and with every bit of patience left in him, Fergusson nodded his head. "Okay, okay. Just what is your grand master plan?"

Chapter 29

Tyler's New Plan

Saturday morning, Tyler drove a rented red pickup truck to Lennon. He checked several venues where Billy might be. When he saw the sign for the homeless shelter, he made a lucky guess that this might be where Billy landed. Outside the Welcome House homeless shelter, Tyler stared at the building trying to figure out the best way to approach finding and taking Billy from the shelter. He figured Billy wouldn't recognize him as anyone from Pittman since Billy was sound asleep when Tyler first spotted him in the Bookworm Shop, so surprise was on his side.

Disguised as a successful businessman, Tyler decided to try the direct approach. The mustache and wig were a great touch, adding to his aura as a rich businessman. Before he climbed the steps, he formulated his reason for being there. Entering the front door, Tyler found a brightly lit entrance with a cheerful young lady at the reception desk, who turned to him and said, "How may I help you, sir?"

"Do you have a person named Billy Wood staying here? Sadie Aboud told me she got your message about Billy Woods on her answering machine," Tyler lied, hoping his lucky guess paid off. "She was sorry she missed you. Since I was coming this way anyway on business, she decided it would be better if someone came to check on Billy rather than just talking to him on the phone. I have a letter from her introducing me and assuring you that I have her permission to meet with Billy Woods," he said. He handed the letter to the receptionist. Fergusson had found Billy's last name when he did his research into Billy's family history. "I'd very much enjoy taking Billy out for pizza or ice cream and seeing how he is adjusting to life here, and where he plans to go from here. By the way, Sadie owns a restaurant where they make excellent pastries. She sent this tray of pastries to thank you for all your trouble and your concern for Billy. Since he came to stay with her, she has become very fond of him." Tyler smiled at the young receptionist.

The receptionist seemed to like him and appeared satisfied with the permission letter. When she went back to check with the caseworker and Billy, Tyler nervously tapped his fingers on the desk. Billy needed to believe and trust him.

The receptionist returned, and said, "Our case worker has been trying to contact Billy's mom and Ms. Aboud with no luck. She's left messages for her to contact the shelter, but no answer. If you wait here, she would like to talk to you."

Thinking fast, Tyler said, "I'm on a tight schedule. I'll be glad to meet with the caseworker when I bring Billy back from lunch. That will give me time to move around a few appointments so I have enough time to speak with her and resolve Billy's situation. I'm hoping that sharing a pizza will help Billy share with me the plans he's made since he took off from Pittman."

"Fine, I hope he opens up to you. He hasn't told us

much. He's very close-mouthed about why he just appeared here on his own," said the receptionist. "What time do you think you and Billy will return?

"It's ten-thirty now. How about one?" said Tyler.

"Good, I'll set up an appointment for one, Mr. ?"

"Mr. Blazure," said Tyler.

Just then the receptionist spotted Billy headed to the cafeteria and called him over. Billy hastened into the room and looked suspiciously at Tyler.

"Ah, Billy, glad to see you. Sadie and Robin send their love. They suggested since I would be in Lennon that I inquire here at the shelter to be sure you were safe. Diane Drew told them that she had driven you to Lennon, and she was very worried about you." Tyler beamed at Billy, believing he presented a persuasive argument.

****

Billy was a bit reluctant to go anywhere with this stranger. He looked familiar, but he couldn't quite place the shaggy-haired man. Since he said Sadie had sent him and had the baked goods to prove it, Billy figured that Tyler was safe, even though he felt uneasy. It concerned him that he had never heard Sadie mention a Mr. Blazure. *Oh well. Pizza is certainly better than shelter food.*

Tyler signed Billy out. "Let's go over to The Pizza Hut on the other side of town. My car is right across the street."

When they got in the car, Tyler seemed nervous, talking fast and sweating. "Are you okay, Mr. Blazure?"

"Sure," said Tyler. "It's very hot today. What's your favorite lunch food?"

Just as Billy started to say, "Pizza with pepperoni and sausage," he noticed Tyler turned the wrong way, away from the other side of town and back toward Pittman. "Where are you going? This isn't the way to Pizza Hut. What's going on? Let me out of this car *now*."

As Billy reached for the handle, he felt a cold, hard steel object sticking into his right shoulder.

"Just stay calm and take your hand off the door handle," said Sam menacingly from the back seat. Billy could tell from the mirror that it was the man who had tried to kidnap him on Wednesday.

Panicked, Billy whispered, "Why are you doing this? What do you want from me?"

Sam laughed. "You'll find out soon enough, but it has to do with the money you're going to turn over to my partners. Now, just sit still and keep quiet. It's only a short ride to the warehouse."

Billy's mind raced, heart beating fast. *What money is he talking about? He can't kill me unless I give him the money I don't know anything about. I need to figure out where they're taking me and how I can get help.*

All those years of touch texting while sitting in class helped Billy as he covertly wrote a message on his phone hoping someone would call him and see this message.

Chapter 30

Billy Is Missing

At the barbeque Saturday, when Billy didn't show up close to dinnertime, everyone was worried. Sadie said, "If there is anything Billy is on time for, it's food. That boy is always hungry."

Asher decided to try Billy's cell phone, and he saw a weird message. "To any band member, this message is for you: Remember the movie, *The Great Escape*. To Ms. George, remember "Fire."To Sadie, remember the poor and homeless."Everyone looked at each other in amazement.

I said, "Why would Billy leave different messages for all of us? Obviously, it was a code of some kind. Why didn't Billy just tell us where he is? Could someone be monitoring his phone? Is he in trouble?"

"What on earth is Billy talking about?" asked Sheriff Houtman.

"You're the sheriff! Obviously, this message contains secret clues," I said sarcastically. Cute as he was, I was getting exasperated with him. "Quit thinking of Billy as a suspect in the crimes on Farley Square and start thinking of him as a victim," I shouted at the stunned Sheriff.

Sheriff Houtman blushed and looked confused.

I was completely unaware of what Mark Houtman

was thinking and interpreted his blushing as anger at me since I implied he was incompetent. I turned to the others. "We need to dissect these messages." My mind was working frantically. *What did Fire, a dragon, have to do with Billy's disappearance? Could he be at the Fire Station?* I quickly made a call to the local fire chief. "Tom, you haven't seen a rather raggedy teenage boy hanging around your station, have you?"

"No," said the fire chief, "it's pretty quiet today."

"Thanks." To the others, I said, "Well, that clue didn't pan out. Billy isn't at the fire station."

Sadie said, "Do you think this clue has anything to do with the key from Billy's pocket?"

"What key?" asked Sheriff Houtman.

Sadie took out the key and handed it to him. "We found this key in Billy's pocket when he first crashed through the door at the bookstore. Do you have any idea what this key could open? We thought it might belong to a safe deposit box or a locker in an airport or bus station."

The sheriff examined the key. "Let me have my deputy check this out. You might be right."

Just then, Lola came back in from the kitchen where she had been trying to get ahold of Fergusson. She had tried his cell, his home number, and the realty office. All calls went to voice mail. "Where do you suppose Fergusson is? Billy and he are both missing. Let's hope they're not together. I don't trust Fergusson. He has a mean side to him. I saw it firsthand when he fired Myrna, yelling and insulting her, and even threatened to toss all her things on the street if she didn't leave immediately. You don't suppose he'll hurt Billy, do you?" Lola asked, tears welling.

Sheriff Houtman tried to calm everyone down. "Relax, everyone. I'm sure Billy is just hiding out from me because he somehow found out about the witness. He knows Myrna can identify him. As for Fergusson, he's a busy man. He's probably just showing real estate to a client."

"What about the secret clues, and why hasn't Billy been at band practice since Thursday afternoon?" shouted Asher. "Myrna just came forward today. Billy couldn't have known about her." Asher was getting pretty worked up and looked ready to charge at Sheriff Houtman.

"The clues are just telling you that Billy knows I'll be looking for him in the bookstore where you were reading the story of Fire, and he was telling Sadie that he loves her, and she should remember him, this poor homeless kid," said Houtman matter-of-factly. "As for the movie *The Great Escape*, he's just being melodramatic. Let's all take a deep breath, eat dinner, and think about where Billy could be hiding out."

No one was in the mood for dinner, but to appease the sheriff, they all sat at the picnic table. Questions abounded. Asher and Mike together said, "I don't think melodrama has anything to do with his reference to *The Great Escape*. What could it mean?"

Mike continued, "And why did he address that clue to the band members? I think he's telling us he's in trouble and needs to escape. He wants us to rescue him."

"If he wants you to rescue him," Sheriff Houtman said, "why wouldn't he have told you where he's hiding?"

"Maybe he's afraid someone will read his

messages on his phone," chimed in Sadie. "Plus, he knows I love him, so why refer to the poor and homeless? No, we're missing something here. You need to stop dismissing this as nothing and start taking us all seriously. We'd love for it all to be so simple, but I am certain Billy is in big trouble."

"As soon as I leave here, I'll confer with Deputy Murphy and figure out how to find Billy in light of your concerns and these text messages. By then, Ferguson should arrive home from any real estate appointments and put your suspicions to rest." Sheriff Houtman made short order of the delicious food in front of him. As he rose to go, he stared at all of us and said, "Remember, we're dealing with a murderer. You all must stand down and leave the investigation to the professionals. I don't want to have to investigate another murder. Stay out of this as of now." With that pronouncement, the sheriff turned and left as we all stared after him.

Chapter 31

How Do We Rescue Billy?

On Sunday, even though the sheriff forcefully forbade it, Mike and Asher took another look at the phone messages they received at the barbeque: "To any band member, this message is for you: Remember the movie, *The Great Escape*. To Ms. George, remember "Fire." To Sadie, remember the poor and homeless."

The boys felt like code breakers as they tried to decipher what Billy meant.

1: *The Great Escape*—Was Billy asking the band members to help him escape? If so, escape from where or from whom?

2: The book, *Fire, the Hiccupping Dragon,* that Billy was so upset about must figure into this. Could Dehlia Wood, the author of the dragon books, have anything to do with his disappearance? Could she have contacted him, and he went to meet her?

3: What do the poor and homeless have to do with anything? Billy may be poor, but is he homeless? No one has seen or heard from his parents.

After mulling this over, Mike and Asher made several leaps of faith. "Mom, we've got it," shouted Asher as he and Mike burst into the bookstore late Sunday afternoon. "Billy is begging us to help him escape, so he must have been kidnapped. If he was kidnapped, it either was by someone homeless, or he is hiding out somewhere in a homeless shelter."

Mike continued their suspicions. "His aunt couldn't have kidnapped him because when we looked to see where she lived, we found out that she died at the beginning of this year. We also couldn't find anything out about his parents. Maybe his parents don't exist, and he lived with this Aunt Dehlia until she died. We need to search all homeless shelters in the area."

"Slow down. Slow down," I said. "We need to call the sheriff and run these conclusions by him. He will have a better idea of how to track down the facts. He also won't appreciate it if we proceed on our own. You heard his warning to keep out of this investigation. We also need to call Sadie. She's sick with worry."

I was sure the boys were onto something, but...

Sheriff Houtman and Sadie arrived at the same time. I immediately summarized the boys' suspicions.

Though the sheriff was put out by our pursuit of clues, even though he warned us off, he had the good sense to realize the boys were onto something.

"I'll have Deputy Murphy check with all homeless shelters in the Berkshire area. I'll get him on it right now," he said as he picked up his phone.

As soon as the sheriff left, I said, "I'll call all my neighbors and see if anyone saw Billy in the last four days."

"Billy let slip that his last name was Wood. We'll search the computer and try to find out about his Aunt Dehlia or anyone named Wood who might be connected to her," said Asher, and he and Mike fired up their computers.

While all this activity was going on, Lola decided

to follow the money because Billy had mentioned the poor. She began a search for the following:

1: Was Dehlia Wood, the author of *Fire, the Hiccupping Dragon*, Billy's Aunt Dehlia? Was Aunt Dehlia rich?

2: If so, who inherited her money when she died?

3: Were Billy's parents rich or poor?

4: Who was Mr. Wood? Was he rich or poor? Billy let slip that he was called Clyde W. Wood and was a mechanic. Could he be Billy's grandfather or Dehlia's?

Sadie, meanwhile, went back to Sweet Indulgences to get some sweets for the busy researchers.

Chapter 32

Another Break-In

After a night of restless sleep, worrying about Billy, Sadie had a feeling of dread when she opened Sweet Indulgences Monday morning. She wasn't sure why her skin was tingling, and her nerves were shooting warnings to her brain. Sadie found out why when the door chime didn't ring as she opened her shop's door. She took a step back after a frantic look of fear crossed her face. Someone had ripped all the posters off the walls, and the smashed door chime in the middle of the floor was surrounded by the shattered glass from the display cases. Shards of glass were everywhere. Printed on the wall in blue icing was "Go back home, foreigner, or else."

Sadie ran out the door, tears streaming down her face, across the street to my Bookworm Shop. She burst in, sobbing, and flung herself at me, collapsing into my outstretched arms.

"Sadie, Sadie," I soothed. "Calm down. It's okay. Whatever happened, we'll take care of it." Lola grabbed a chair for Sadie to sit on and went in search of a wet cloth to wipe Sadie's face and some tea to calm her down. We both stared at Sadie, waiting for her to say something. When Sadie could get words out between her sobs, she told us what she saw when she opened the front door to her store.

"Thank goodness Aunt Florence asked me to open today. I don't think her heart could handle a shock like this. Do you think ISIS sympathizers have come to Pittman?"

"No, Sadie, I'm sure it's not ISIS. They wouldn't have called you a foreigner and told you to go home. It's just some horrid, prejudiced person or persons. I'm sure Mopey Tyler had a hand in this."

"We must call the sheriff," said Lola.

"I suspect you'd better. He will never forgive me if anyone hurts Sadie," I said.

When Sheriff Houtman arrived, he took one look at Sadie, dropped to his knees, and took her into his arms. "I'm here. No one is going to hurt you. You're going to be okay."

Lola and I stared at him, then we looked at each other in amazement. We had never seen robot man show a bit of emotion. Maybe his feelings for Sadie were deeper than anyone suspected.

Sheriff Mark Houtman rose and looked at Lola and me with tears in his eyes. Then his look turned to one of rage. "What is going on around here? Murder, vandalism, robberies, arson, disappearances, and now more threats of violence. Whoever did this is going to pay. I am not going to stand by and let Sadie or anyone else get hurt."

Mark Houtman, man transformed, gently helped Sadie from her chair. "Sadie, are you up to showing me the store so I can look for evidence of who may have broken in?"

Sadie nodded weakly. With the support of the sheriff, they crossed the street to Sweet Indulgences.

Lola and I locked up the bookstore and followed them.

Chapter 33

To the Rescue

As we headed toward Sweet Indulgences, I was getting anxious. "This break-in at Sadie's restaurant might have something to do with Billy's disappearance since no one has heard from him since Friday," I whispered to Lola. "If someone is willing to vandalize a store, painting such vile comments on the walls, what will they be willing to do to Billy if they have him in their custody?"

I decided we had to convince Sheriff Houtman that Billy was not the vandal who destroyed Sweet Indulgences and the other stores on Farley Square. We also needed to show a connection to other suspects rather than Billy. Surely, Billy's disappearance will convince the sheriff that Billy did nothing wrong. Maybe now he'll take some interest in the note Billy sent to the boys.

After Sheriff Houtman surveyed the damage to Sadie's shop and went back to his office, I set up a meeting at my Bookworm Shop for that afternoon when the boys came home from school. When my crew was gathered, I took charge. "Billy must be frightened, or he would have called us. Billy cares for Sadie and would never hurt her by destroying her shop. Sheriff's warning or not, we have to find Billy since the sheriff has been so ineffective, and we need to find out who trashed Sweet Indulgences.

"Here's my plan. Feel free to add any suggestions. Asher and Mike, you need to find out where Fergusson and Tyler were on Sunday night. They haven't been seen lately, so not only is Billy missing, but so are they. Mike, you need to find out your dad's connection to Fergusson and Tyler. Where was he on Sunday? Figure out where Tyler and Fergusson have been lately, and what they might be up to. Dig into their past; see if they knew each other before landing in Pittman and if they are in any way connected to Billy's disappearance or the killing or vandalism, but be careful. Sadie, you need to sweet talk Sheriff Houtman. Offer to go out with him on a date, whatever it takes. Try to convince him this is serious. Cry if you must or bully him by showing him who's boss. We must get Billy off the sheriff's radar.

"Lola and I will question the neighbors and see if anyone saw Billy on Friday. Maybe someone gave him a ride somewhere, or he took a bus. If we find out where he went, we will go there and call to update everyone. If no one finds Billy, we'll compare notes when we meet again. Also, we'll ask the neighbors if anyone saw any suspicious characters near Sweet Indulgences this morning or last night. See if anyone has any security cameras that might have captured the break-ins."

"Everyone gather here tomorrow tonight at eight after our shops close and the boys are through with band practice. Sadie, you should invite Sheriff Houtman to the gathering as well." I sent them on their way. The boys would have to hurry to make their searches before they headed back to school. Sadie stayed with me as she finished her coffee. She was thoughtful now. Once again, she was the fierce fighter against ISIS, determined to survive.

I, on the other hand, didn't feel brave or competent to solve this crime. My husband would have searched everywhere for the perpetrator, but I felt paralyzed. I am a businesswoman and a mother, not a brave detective. Why can't the deputy and sheriff do their jobs?

I expressed everyone's deepest fears. "Could Billy be dead? Could he have just run away? The vandalism and racial slurs were so cruel. I'm sure it had to be Tyler. I don't know anyone else mean enough to pull this off. He's always calling you a foreigner in that derogatory way of his." Frustrated, I put my head in my hands and took a deep breath.

Sadie said, "I am so afraid that someone has hurt Billy. I can't lose him. I've lost one brother already, and I won't lose another boy I care about. As for Tyler, if he trashed my store, he'll wish he never met me. May the wrath of the Lebanese be upon him."

Sadie stood up and said, "Robin, I'm going to go and call that inflexible sheriff and invite him to lunch tomorrow. Somehow, we'll get him to listen to us and take action."

After school, Asher and Mike went home to further research Tyler and Fergusson's pasts. They were going to question all the owners of the shops on Farley Square to find out if any of them had seen Fergusson or Tyler in the past twenty-four hours.

Fergusson, they found, had owned Welcome Realty for about three years, but the boys were having a hard time tracing his past. He got his realty license ten years ago, worked at Star Realty in Chicago for two years, left there, and they could not find any evidence of where he had been for the intervening five years. His realty license was current, but where had he gone after he left Star Realty? Asher called Star Realty, but the woman who answered had only worked there a year and had no knowledge of Fergusson. Asher asked to speak to the owner, but Mr. Stein wouldn't be in until Wednesday morning. Asher made an appointment for Mike and him to talk to Mr. Stein by phone at his office on Wednesday afternoon.

Mike, meanwhile, was researching Tyler. He traced Tyler to Chicago also where he had received numerous traffic tickets, but he was arrested four years ago for drug trafficking. Since it was Tyler's first offense in Chicago, he was let off with two months of jail time and a year of community service.

There were other questions the boys needed to get answered:

1 Could Fergusson also have been in jail during his missing five-year time? Why?

2 Was Tyler still dealing drugs as they all suspected? Could the person who testified against him in Chicago have moved to Pittman? Could that person be the murder victim?

3 A horrible question occurred to the boys. Lola had spent some time in Chicago before she went off to California to pursue her acting career. Could Lola have met Tyler or Fergusson or the victim from the Bluegrass band? Much as the boys liked Lola, no one seemed to know much about her personal life. Could she have been involved with drugs during her time in Chicago or LA?

4 Did Tyler and Fergusson know each other before coming to Pittman? If so, how did they meet?

5 Why did both men decide to open businesses in Pittman?

6 Did anyone else in Pittman, besides maybe Lola, have a prior connection to Tyler or Fergusson?

7 Why do Tyler and Fergusson seem so chummy with Sam, Mike's dad?

Sam had been in prison with Frank. Could they have met Tyler or Fergusson while they were there?

The boys planned to run these questions when they all meet at Sweet Indulgences tomorrow night.

Chapter 34

Too Many Suspects

When Sheriff Houtman and Deputy Murphy returned to the office, the sheriff composed his Murder Board of Suspects for the murder of Bobby Jo Love, the victim in the alley, listing each suspect's alibi, opportunity, and motive. They also needed to find who vandalized the shops and if anyone was responsible for Billy's disappearance. The sheriff and Murphy brainstormed opportunities, motives, and any evidence pointing to each suspect.

EVIDENCE:

1 Trophy found by Bobby Jo's body is a band trophy. Who had access to the trophy?

2 Murphy confirms two sets of fingerprints on the trophy, Mike's, and Billy's. Since these are the only fingerprints, did the killer wear gloves, or was Mike or Billy the killer?

3 Time of death—sometime on Friday night or early Saturday morning according to the coroner's report

4 Place of death—alley behind The Joker's Den

MIKE:

Alibi-Fingerprints on trophy because he won it last week at the Band Banquet

Trophy displayed at Ten Pins Bowling Alley so

anyone could have access to it

Opportunity—Seen in Joker's Den on Wednesday.

Could have been casing the store figuring out how and where to kill Tyler, and instead killed one of his customers

Motive—Hated how Tyler treated Robin and Sadie who had been so good to him

Thought he could kill Love, a customer of The Joker's Den, and blame the murder on Tyler

BILLY:

Alibi—Missing? Might have faked kidnapping

Opportunity—Had time to plan a murder.

His fingerprints were on the band trophy also.

Motive—?

LOLA:

Alibi—??? Need to question her

Opportunity—??? Manages to be missing when we question suspects

Unknown past. Why Pittman?

Motive—Victim might have sold lethal drugs to her mom

Need to see if her mom has any connection to the band

ASHER:

Alibi—???

Opportunity—???

Motive—Tyler hates Asher's mom and treats her terribly.

Might have wanted to ruin Tyler's business since many of his customers would vanish if a murder occurred at The Joker's Den.

ROBIN:

Alibi—???

Opportunity—???

Motive—Robin has quite a temper as I recently witnessed.

She has been researching Tyler. Maybe she acted to ruin Tyler and avenge his actions against Sadie and the boys.

SADIE:

Alibi—Why would Sadie vandalize her own shop? But the vandal and killer could be two separate people.

Opportunity—Has skills she learned to protect her family from ISIS

Owns a gun so she's willing to kill

Motive—Could the victim be a member of ISIS here to track down Sadie?

Please don't let it be Sadie, Mark thought.

FERGUSSON:

Alibi—???

Opportunity—Had a key to The Joker's Den

Motive—Money! If Tyler went to jail for murder, no more partnership

Why a 5-year gap in Fergusson's history? Did he know Tyler during that time? Did he know Bobby Jo, the victim?

SAM:

Alibi—The Ten Pins Bowling Alley closes at 11:00 p.m. Would Sam have time to murder the victim?

Opportunity—Access to murder weapon

Motive—Money. Could blackmail Tyler for killing the kid

FRANK:

Alibi—Need to find out if Sam or Frank closed up at 11

Opportunity—Access to murder weapon

Motive—Did he know the victim from Chicago?

UNKNOWN DRUG CUSTOMER:

Alibi—Unknown ???

Opportunity—Many unsavory characters had been seen shopping at The Joker's Den.

Motive—Self-defense

Maybe Tyler refused to sell this person drugs, and the person attacked Tyler

Wrong place, wrong time

Murphy and I looked at each other. "There are just too many suspects. Let's take a break and grab some coffee. My mind is swimming."

Chapter 35

Determining a Murderer

As he sipped his much-needed coffee, Sheriff Houtman was flustered and knew he needed a plan of action. They had too many suspects and too many motives for Bobby Jo's murder. Not only did he need to solve the murder, but he still needed to determine who vandalized the stores. Was he looking for one culprit or two or a gang?

His gut told him to rule out Asher and Mike because they are likable and decent kids. Though they had easy access to the murder weapon, the band trophy, they didn't seem like the type to commit a murder.

He eliminated Robin. She's an amateur detective and a busybody, but he knows she's also a loving mother and a well-respected member of the community.

His heart said to eliminate Sadie, but she was the only one with a known killer- instinct, but she owns a gun and will use it if threatened.

"We also need to know the facts of Billy's disappearance. Could he have murdered Billy Jo? Why? Where is Billy? Why did he disappear? It's Monday, and no one has seen Billy since Thursday," the sheriff said to Murphy. "If we eliminate Asher, Mike, and Robin, that leaves Sadie, Billy, Lola, Tyler, Fergusson, Sam, and Frank. You investigate Billy's background and the kidnapping. Also, find out more about Mike's dad and his employee, Frank. I think they both were in prison at the same time. Check it out. I'll cover the rest. I want to know more about Lola. I know Ms. George trusts her, but does she deserve such blind trust? We'll meet later today."

Chapter 36

Captive Billy

As the masked kidnapper held a gun on Billy in the truck, Billy felt in his pocket and found a piece of band music from practice. He managed to tear it into tiny pieces, hoping someone from the band would spot the music score. As Sam forced him out of the truck, Billy carefully tossed the pieces on the ground as he kicked and screamed and was forced up the steps of the warehouse. He managed to get a hand free and punched Sam. Angry, Sam threw Billy forward, tossing him to the floor. As Billy got up, Sam forced him into a chair and taped him securely to it.

"You stay right there and keep quiet. No one will hear you screaming in this abandoned warehouse. Someone will return in an hour with papers for you to sign. Be ready to sign over your inheritance from your Aunt Dehlia or be ready to die," snarled Sam.

What inheritance? Sign over what? How do they know Aunt Dehlia? I don't understand what he's talking about. He has to know Ms. George if he knows about Aunt Dehlia's books. Just like when he was younger, Billy didn't know who to turn to. He started to go into himself and began to remember all the bad things that had happened to him when he was younger.

His dad was killed in a drive-by shooting in a bad

section of Chicago when Billy was only four. Billy's mom went into a deep depression and decided she couldn't take on the responsibility of being a single mom.

One cold winter day, she packed up their belongings, drove down Lake Shore Drive, out of the city, and didn't stop until she reached Indiana. Billy didn't understand what was going on. "We're going on a traveling adventure," his mom said. "We're going to see Gram and Pop at their farm."

Billy was excited. "How far is the farm? Do they have a cow? Can I milk it? Do they have a horse? Can I ride it?"

"Stop asking questions," his mom shouted. "Can't you ever be quiet?"

It was silent in the warehouse, and his memories seemed so vivid. *Why do I only remember bad things about my parents? But I can remember good things about my grandparents.*

The sign out front said, "Clyde's Dairy Farm." His mom pulled up in front of the wooden house. Just as they were getting out of the car, Gram and Pop came running out to the porch shouting and hollering, "Nellie, Billy? Wow, what a surprise. Billy, get up here and give your Gram and Pop a big hug."

Never had it felt so good to be held. He cried as Gram kissed him again and again, and then Pop ruffled his hair and kept patting his back.

That night, Billy's mom left, and he never saw her again.

Frightened and exhausted, Billy fell asleep.

Chapter 37

Who to Believe

Saturday afternoon as he was waking up from his troubled nap, Billy heard banging on the warehouse stairs. Putting dreams aside, he began to struggle with the tape on his wrists. Tyler and Fergusson entered the room. Billy recognized Fergusson as the owner of Welcome Realty. He wasn't surprised that Mopey Tyler would be Fergusson's partner in crime.

After Tyler entered, he walked up to Billy. "Now, Billy," he said in a menacing tone, "here is paper and pen. Write what I dictate to you."

"Wait a minute. Just wait a minute," shouted Billy. "Who are you to threaten me? If my Aunt Dehlia left me an inheritance, where did she get the money, and why should I give any of it to you? I always thought Aunt Dehlia was a great storyteller, but I had no idea she made money from writing a bunch of children's books. How did you arrive at this stupid conclusion, and what right do you have to make demands?"

Tyler wasn't one to tolerate someone yelling at him. As soon as Fergusson saw Tyler raise his hand, he stopped him and took him aside. He told Tyler they needed to calm Billy down if he were ever to write a coherent letter that would hold up to lawyer Wright's scrutiny. Wright already seemed a bit suspicious because Billy wouldn't come in person. Fergusson had a hard time restraining Tyler, but Tyler finally gave in to Fergusson's logic.

"Okay, Billy, we've talked to your Aunt Dehlia's lawyer. We told him we found you, but you didn't want any part of owning the rights to your Aunt's books," said Fergusson. "We owe you an explanation and understand your confusion."

"You sure do owe me an explanation and much more," Billy snapped back.

"Look, Billy," said Fergusson reasonably, "let me explain. We're just protecting you. Your Aunt Dehlia is worth millions, and we found out recently that her estate lawyer was looking for you because she willed you all her fortune when she died. All we want is to take care of this vast fortune for you to make sure no one takes advantage of you. I am a whiz in finance and am willing to advise you as to which investments would be the wisest. Tyler has a flair for business, so if you allow us, we will gladly help you keep your inheritance safe and away from predators who want to take advantage of your lack of expertise. Maybe we overreacted by bringing you to this warehouse, but—"

"Bringing me? Bringing me? You mean kidnapping me and holding a gun to my head," shouted Billy.

At this point, Fergusson knew he couldn't become his money manager if Billy didn't trust him.

Maybe this was the wrong way to have approached the kid.

Chapter 38

Billy Concocts a Plan of His Own

After realizing Billy was missing, Mike and Asher hurried to the bookstore after school Monday. "We've found out several things today."

"So has the sheriff," I replied. "Deputy Murphy tracked down a homeless shelter in Lennon. Diane Drew picked Billy up while he was hitchhiking Thursday and gave him a ride to the shelter. When Murphy contacted the Director of the Shelter, she was quite upset and told the Deputy that late Saturday morning a man in a red pickup said that he was a friend of Sadie and mine, and he took Billy out for pizza. This Mr. Blazure was supposed to meet with the director when they finished lunch but never returned with Billy. He gave a false name, but when the Director described him to Deputy Murphy, the description matched Mopey Tyler."

"Wow. Where do you think Tyler took Billy, and why? It's been over two days and still no word from Billy since his cryptic message," said Asher.

"The sheriff is looking for Tyler now. What's your news?"

"Lola was following the money, and she saw several large transfers to Tyler and one to Sam from Fergusson. We wondered why Fergusson would give them money. Mike asked his dad why, and he just got mad and shouted, 'Mind your own business, you nosy kid, or you could get hurt just like Billy.' Then Sam stormed out of Ten Pins."

"Oh no, has Tyler hurt Billy?" cried Sadie. "We have to tell Sheriff Houtman about Sam's threat."

Just then, Mike's phone rang. After talking to the caller, Mike said, "That was Larry, our bass player in the band. He and his buddies were in the warehouse district running an errand for his dad, and they saw the strangest thing. A bunch of scraps of paper was blowing all over the sidewalk. It looked like they had music on them. Larry picked several pieces up and recognized the music as a piece we play in the band. Curious, the other band members gathered up all the pieces and confirmed that it was a march we were playing in the upcoming band competition. Larry wrote down the addresses of all the warehouses surrounding the torn paper site."

Mike looked at Sadie, Asher, and me. "This might be the clue that Billy addressed to the band members in his message. Should we tell the sheriff and have him search the warehouses for Billy?"

I hurriedly called Sheriff Houtman, but both he and his deputy were out of the office. His receptionist said they went to The Joker's Den. I asked her to have him stop at the bookstore or call me as soon as possible. He needed to get to the warehouse district immediately.

Sadie decided to act now, and she took the two boys and Lola and headed to the warehouse district. "We'll find Billy. Send the sheriff as soon as you get ahold of him," Sadie said.

"Be careful," I said. "It could be dangerous. We're

dealing with a possible murderer."

"Don't worry, Robin. I have my gun. Nobody is going to mess with us or Billy."

Somehow, knowing that Sadie had her gun didn't calm me down or make me less worried. The image of one vengeful lady with a gun, one emotional actress, and two impulsive teenagers didn't calm me down either. "Okay, but promise me you won't do anything if you find them until the sheriff gets there."

Sadie answered something as they flew out the door, but I wasn't sure it was a promise.

Chapter 39

Fugitive

Fergusson returned to the warehouse Sunday morning and convinced Billy to write the letter to the lawyer, making Fergusson his guardian over financial affairs. "I assure you, Billy, that this is in your best interest. If you have a problem with trusting Tyler, he doesn't have to be a part of this. I can discuss this with Ms. George if you would like. She needs to be made aware of Lola and Sadie's plot to steal your inheritance."

Billy was still suspicious, but he decided to go ahead with the letter, get Fergusson to release him, and hopefully talk to the sheriff and Ms. George to see if Fergusson took the letter Monday morning to his lawyer. Ms. George should be able to set him right about all this. Asher certainly loved his mother, and Billy trusted Asher, so he would put his trust in Ms. George's judgement. Fergusson handed the letter from the lawyer to Billy for him to sign agreeing to make Fergusson the financial administrator of his estate.

"I'll give this letter to my friend Judge Parker late today and have him draw up the proper guardianship papers. They should be ready for us to pick up Tuesday morning. Until then, you should stay here in the warehouse, safe from Lola, or Sadie, in case they get wind of these transactions and want to harm you. I'll take care of Tyler." Fergusson took out a bag. "Here, I brought you dinner. Eat, then sleep. You've been through a lot. I won't let anyone hurt you or take advantage of you, Billy." With that statement, Fergusson left.

Come Monday morning, once he left the judge's office, Fergusson made a trip to the bank. He transferred most of the money in his business account to a bank in Brazil, explaining to the bank manager that he was leaving to execute a major business deal in South America and needed ready access to his business account. He took out nine thousand dollars from his personal account for expenses for the trip. He left money in both his personal and business account so no one would become suspicious. When the inheritance money comes through, he can just deposit it in either account and then request a transfer from Brazil.

As Fergusson was leaving, the manager said, "Have a successful trip."

"Oh, I will," Fergusson said.

After leaving the bank, he went to Welcome Realty to collect his important papers and deeds to his various properties from his safe. He knew he needed to leave Pittman and get out of the immediate area before the sheriff came to arrest him.

How I hate this town and everyone in it.

Fergusson remembered his dealings with Tyler, Sam, and Frank when he lived in Chicago. He had been hopeful these men would be his friends.

One of his first real estate transactions in Chicago was the purchase of Tyler's store when Tyler was sent to prison. When Fergusson went to the jail to ask Tyler some questions about the business, he first met Sam, a prisoner who had befriended Tyler. Fergusson made many trips to the prison to work out details of various shady deals with Tyler and often talked to Sam and his cellmate Frank, who seemed like a decent guy who had been in the wrong place at the wrong time and got caught. Fergusson liked Sam and Frank and thought he might be able to involve Sam or Frank in future shady schemes.

When Tyler and he planned Billy's kidnapping, Fergusson knew he could make Sam take part because he could hold Sam's felony over him and threaten him that he'd inform the parole board that Sam was not keeping to his conditions of parole, namely no drinking and no hanging out with drug dealers. He needed Sam to take part because he needed to have a fall guy in case the kidnapping plans went south. Fergusson could blame Sam for the kidnapping and give Tyler and himself time to escape town with Aunt Dehlia's money. Since he wanted to keep the people in the know to a minimum, and because Frank had said he would never again go to prison, Fergusson told Sam to keep Frank out of the loop just in case he would go to the sheriff and squeal about the kidnapping plot. Frank didn't strike Fergusson as someone who would get involved in any shady deal.

Fergusson found out that Tyler was involved with the killing of Bobby Jo, the murder victim in the alley. Tyler confessed all this to Fergusson Saturday night after they returned from the warehouse where they were holding Billy.

Fergusson was furious when he heard Tyler's confession. This would kill all their plans if the sheriff found out.

Tyler confessed that "Bobby Jo threatened he would expose me as a drug supplier in Chicago. Bobby Jo hated me because I sold drugs to Lola's mom, who was a mentor to Bobby Jo in Lovey Doves' Bluegrass Band. Bobby Jo told me he had been traveling around the Berkshires searching for me, and, by chance, spotted me laughing with friends on the lawn at Tanglewood during a Boston Symphony Concert, where they were playing the score from "West Side Story". Who would have thought such trouble would arise from attending a simple performance? Bobby Jo said he followed me from Tanglewood to Pittman and then to The Joker's Den.

"When Bobby Jo came inside, he threatened me that unless I gave him one hundred thousand dollars, he would expose my past and present illegal activity to the sheriff and all the merchants on Farley Square. That would ruin not only my business but my reputation as well.

"I had to act fast so I agreed to the payment and said, 'Bobby Jo, meet me in the alley behind The Joker's Den at ten p.m. after I close my shop. That will give me time to get your money, but this is a one-time payment. You try to bleed any more money out of me, and you're a dead man.'

"Bobby Jo wasn't afraid of me. He warned me that if I tried anything, he could easily overpower me because he was an accomplished wrestler.

"When Bobby Jo turned and left, I knew I had to get rid of him, so I went to Ten Pins for a drink to boost my courage. While there, I poured out my troubles to Frank, who always was a sympathetic listener. Frank listened as I explained my plan for getting rid of Bobby Jo. Frank seemed agitated by my revelation. With shaking hands, Frank was getting me another drink when I spotted Mike's band trophy displayed on the bar. I made a quick decision.

"As I left Ten Pins, I covertly grabbed the trophy. I went back to The Joker's Den and filled a satchel with newspaper. At ten p.m. Friday, I locked my store, stepped into the alley, and handed Bobby Jo the satchel. Bobby Jo said, 'I'm glad to see you're being wise. This will be the one and only payment I ask for as promised.' As Bobby Jo went to open the bag, I raised the band trophy and savagely struck him on his right temple. I knew he would soon be dead as he lay bleeding profusely on the ground, so I hightailed it out of the alley and headed home. I needed an escape plan in case they traced the murder to me. I laid awake most of the night trying to think coherently.

"If the sheriff finds out about my drug deals, he could put me back in the slammer. I've done you a favor, Fergusson. I'm sure Bobby Jo would have found out about the kidnapping and blackmailed you and Sam also. You don't have to thank me. Just execute your escape plan and get us both far from Pittman before Robin, Sadie, or the sheriff put two and two together and come looking for me or you."

"Tyler, calm down. Let's take a bit to think this through logically. Right now, no one is going to suspect you of killing an unknown vagrant. The sheriff knows that someone committed the robberies and trashed the stores. A vagrant is the perfect fall guy for those crimes. Perhaps his partner decided to get rid of him so he wouldn't have to share in the profits. If the sheriff buys that excuse, it throws all suspicion off you or any of us here in Pittman."

"I need money now," demanded Tyler. "I repeat; I'm not going back to jail."

Fergusson realized Tyler was becoming unhinged. He would have to get rid of Tyler, but how? Perhaps he should just give him money and send him off to his island with a promise to join him soon. If Tyler is stuck on a tropical island, he would be in a jail of his own making. Tyler would be blamed for Bobby Jo's killing and could never return. Fergusson was quite sure he could concoct a convincing argument to blame Tyler for Billy's kidnapping also and tell the sheriff that he was only involved because Tyler threatened to kill him if he didn't participate.

Fergusson also played with the idea of killing Tyler and then producing evidence of his masterminding Billy's kidnapping and killing Bobby Jo. He could then blame Sam for Tyler's killing. He needed time to think.

"For now, Tyler, go back to the Joker's Den and carry on as if nothing has happened. If anyone asks about your whereabouts last night, tell them you were with me, and that we had supper and played cards until about one a.m., and then you went home to bed. I'll vouch for your alibi. Above all else, stay calm. Meanwhile, I'll get the money together for you in case you need to flee in a hurry. If that happens, I'll get you out of here and join you later as soon as I can get my paperwork in order."

Fergusson believed by paying Sam and Tyler a generous share of Aunt Dehlia's inheritance, they would want to be his partner for any future deals. Wrong. Sam made a point that Tyler was his partner in their original blackmail scheme but said he would be glad to switch sides and instead become Fergusson's partner. Fergusson didn't trust Sam now. How did he know Sam wouldn't turn the tables on him also? If Fergusson didn't make Sam a partner, he threatened to blackmail Fergusson for skipping town and running from fraud charges pertaining to all his shady real estate dealings in Chicago.

Fergusson agreed and knew he had to convince Sam that Tyler was the problem.

"Sam, if you can get rid of Tyler, everything will be fine. I'll include you as my partner in all future business dealings." Fergusson had to move fast to get out of town before Sam got rid of Tyler.

"Okay. That sounds fair," said Sam. "Maybe I can plant evidence that Tyler killed Bobby Jo, then Tyler will either be arrested or flee town."

Now the plot to get the inheritance is down the drain, mourned Fergusson. *Too many things are stacking up against me. Everything is unraveling. When Billy is freed, he will identify me as one of the kidnappers. The sheriff will not buy my excuse that Tyler and I were saving Billy from Lola and Sadie's devious plan to bilk Billy out of his inheritance. The stupid sheriff is so enamored of that foreigner he won't believe any alibi that accuses his Sadie of wrong. If Sam manages to kill Tyler, that will make everything more manageable. The sheriff will also blame Sam for the kidnapping, and I'll be home free, but then again, Billy will identify me. I need to leave town and fast, or I need to dispose of Billy before he is found.*

Fergusson booked a flight out of Albany for Tuesday. This would give him plenty of time to tie all the loose ends together, but still far away when the sheriff figured out his role in the kidnapping.

I can transfer the balance from my accounts when I get to Brazil, then I will begin to live the good life.

Chapter 40

A Second Murder

All weekend, Tyler kept looking over his shoulder for any sign of the sheriff. He heard all the rumors spreading through the town. Pittman was a safe town so everyone was speculating about how a murderer could kill someone here in this idyllic setting. Tyler came to Fergusson Monday morning in quite a state. "I hardly slept all weekend," Tyler said. "Have you figured out our plan of action?"

Having decided to do away with Tyler, Fergusson convinced Tyler to go to The Joker's Den and get whatever he would need to start his new life in South America. "Also, go home and pack clothes for a cruise and a life of leisure. That's what we will have soon. I'll then meet you tonight at The Joker's Den to make our getaway. It's better to leave under cover of darkness. Meanwhile, I'll arrange everything."

"Okay, okay, that sounds good. This nightmare should soon be over, I hope," said Tyler. "I'll meet you in The Joker's Den at about nine o'clock tonight. Then we'll drive to Boston, get a flight to Miami, and take a cruise ship to tour the Caribbean Islands, then on to South America. I'll bring travel brochures, and we can decide which city appeals to each of us. We'll have plenty of time on the ship to decide where we'll enjoy our idyllic retirement."

At eight o'clock Monday night, Fergusson put his murder plan into action. He had decided it would be better if he got rid of Tyler rather than involve a second person like Sam. He wasn't sure Sam had the courage to kill Tyler. Fergusson left his office before their scheduled meet-up time, used his key, and opened the darkened Joker's Den. He hid behind the cash register counter, waiting for Tyler. Fergusson knew Tyler would arrive early because he would be eager to get on the road as soon as darkness arrived. Fergusson heard the creek of the turning door handle at about eight o'clock. When Tyler entered and dropped his suitcases on the floor next to the door, Fergusson readied himself for the kill. Trophy in hand, he was about to step out from behind the counter when he heard some footsteps and a voice boom out, "Tyler, you scumbag, you deserve to die."

Chapter 41

Trouble at The Joker's Den

Tuesday, I decided to go in search of the sheriff. I needed to talk to him about all the ideas running around in my head. He just seemed focused on the wrong suspects, and I needed to nudge him in a different direction.

As I was passing The Joker's Den, I saw a line of unsavory characters outside the door of the store. A man with a scruffy beard called out, "Hey, Tyler, open up. It's getting hot out here."The crowd was milling about averting their eyes from the police who were converging on the store. The customers kept knocking on the door, yelling and chanting, "Tyler, Tyler, Tyler, open the door."

I stopped at the pharmacy and asked Mr. Klette what was going on.

He said, "I called Sheriff Houtman because I didn't like the fact people in line were getting quite rowdy, and their shouting was frightening my customers."

When the sheriff arrived, Deputy Murphy said, "Everyone, step aside and calm down."

He then called Fergusson to get a key to The Joker's Den that Tyler rented from him. When he finally reached him on his cell, Fergusson brought the key. The sheriff and Deputy Murphy cautiously entered

The Joker's Den. They flipped on the lights, locked the outside door behind them, and methodically checked the front of the store. The door to the back storage room was closed, so the two of them entered cautiously, guns drawn.

Murphy was headed to the closet on the right side of the storage room when he heard Sheriff Houtman's shaky voice. "Murphy, over here."

Murphy hurried to where the sheriff was pointing. "Oh no." Murphy flinched.

There was Mopey Tyler, with the back of his head bashed in, dried blood matting his dark hair and covering the tile floor under his head. Sheriff Houtman felt for a nonexistent pulse then said, "Murphy, call the coroner. Tyler is dead, most likely murder. I know many people hated him, but I can't think of anyone evil enough to kill him. We now have two murders in our sleepy town. I should have stayed in Boston."

Sheriff Houtman continued, "Let's see if the coroner can determine a time of death. Have the coroner bag everything to send to the forensic lab in Albany. Seal off this store. No one gets in or out until we process everything. There is a trophy next to his body that probably is the murder weapon. It also looks just like the band trophy used to murder Bobby Jo. I wonder if we are dealing with a serial killer. Bag the trophy and take it to the station. We'll compare the two trophies. After you get it processed for fingerprints, bring it back to Farley Square and show the trophy to all the band members and the people in the shops. Someone has to recognize a trophy as distinctive as this one."

Scratching his head, Sheriff Houtman said to

Deputy Murphy, "You know the locals well. Who do you think would want to kill Mopey Tyler?"

Murphy answered, "I think you might be surprised that you will end up with a sizeable list of people with motives. Tyler wasn't exactly a popular person. Ever since he came to Pittman, he's managed to make enemies without really trying."

Chapter 42

Have We Finally Found Billy?

Early Tuesday morning, Sadie and her gang of rescuers set out for the warehouse district. They began canvassing each warehouse. Two of them looked completely abandoned.

Sadie called Robin. "We have the addresses that Larry, Asher's friend from the band, copied down, so now we're going to try to get into the abandoned warehouses and search for Billy. Has the sheriff surfaced yet? Are we going to get him to join us in our search?"

"Sadie," Robin said, "there's been a horrible development. Mopey Tyler has been killed. That's where Sheriff Houtman and Deputy Murphy have been. Rumor is that Tyler was killed in his Joker's Den last night or early this morning. There's a huge crowd of spectators on the street in front of his shop. Deputy Murphy has pushed everyone back and is roping off the sidewalk in front and the alley behind Tyler's store. You'd better get back here. We'll have Sheriff Houtman do the checking of the abandoned warehouses. Things are too dangerous with two murders now for you all to be snooping around. You might end up face to face with a murderer."

Sadie would have objected that she could take care

of herself, but she wasn't alone. Even though she wasn't afraid, she felt responsible for Asher, Mike, and Lola, and she vividly remembered what happened to her brother.

"Everyone, we need to return to Farley Square. There've been some sinister and worrisome developments," Sadie said as she shooed the bewildered investigators into her car.

Chapter 43

Under Arrest?

After several hours processing the crime scene at
The Joker's Den, a frustrated Mark Houtman came in
the door at Sweet Indulgences. Sadie immediately went
to him and said, "Oh Sheriff, we heard about Tyler's
murder. How awful. Sit down and take a breath. You
could use a break for some hot chocolate and chocolate
chip cookies."

"Sadie, this isn't a social call," said the Sheriff
through gritted teeth. "Robin George and Sadie Aboud,
I'd like you to come down to the station to answer
questions about the murder of Mopey, I mean Thomas
Tyler."

I jumped out of my seat. "What? Are you crazy?
What kind of questions? What could you think Sadie
and I know about his murder? I didn't even know he
was dead until I saw the crowd, and Sadie wasn't even
here. She was doing your job searching for Billy. What
is going on? I can't believe you want to question us
when there's a murderer on the loose and Billy is still
missing." My face flamed with anger.

"Robin, calm down. I just want to ask you some
questions," said the flustered sheriff.

"Are we under arrest?" I shot back.

"No, not yet."

"Not yet? Why you incompetent…"

Sadie put her hand on my arm to stop me from saying anything else I might regret.

I took a deep breath and said, "If we are not under arrest, we are not going down to the station. If you want to question us, you can do so in Sadie's office. If you would prefer to arrest us, we won't answer a single question until, and if, our lawyer advises us to talk to you."

Sadie was petrified and just stared at me and the sheriff.

I turned to Sadie. "This is America. We have rights. This is our elected sheriff, not an interrogator from ISIS."

Sadie was pale and shaking. The only man she had trusted since leaving Lebanon was Mark Houtman, and here he was, believing she might be a murderer.

"You'll be okay," I comforted. "Our esteemed sheriff should be ashamed of his conduct." I was fuming.

Sadie just put her hands in her apron pockets and tried to stop shaking. She kept looking at the pictures on the wall that showed many happy customers licking ice cream off their smiling lips. She couldn't look at Mark Houtman.

Sheriff Houtman appeared baffled. Not sure how to handle us, he caved in. "Okay, okay. You don't have to come down to the station. I'll question you here. Deputy Murphy can bring the murder weapon here to see if either of you recognize it."

"You have the murder weapon? When did Tyler die?" Starting toward the Sheriff, I shouted, "Why are Sadie and I suspects in Tyler's death? Who are your other suspects? Have you looked at motives or alibis, or are you just hoping to solve this murder through intimidation," I threw out at him, who by now most likely was wishing he was back in his quiet office. He couldn't even look at Sadie's sad, defeated face and her slumped shoulders. `

"Robin, I'm not trying to intimidate anyone. You are a suspect because of your rancorous association with Tyler. Sadie, you're a suspect because of your hatred for Tyler due to the insults he threw at you and the fact that he intimidated you. We found out that he is the one who trashed your shop and wrote those vile threats on your walls, so you might be seeking revenge," he said. "There are also other suspects. We just need to interview everyone."

"Who else are suspects?" I asked.

"I understand Lola worked in his office under false pretenses. Her dad's downfall was caused by drugs and alcohol, and her mom died from a drug overdose, so she hates anyone associated with dealing drugs, and Tyler is certainly suspected of drug trafficking though we hadn't been able to gather enough evidence to arrest him. She also has a connection to the murder of Bobby Jo Love, the Bluegrass band member. He was a member of Lola's Mom's band."

Sadie and I were both surprised at this connection. Lola hadn't given any indication that she knew the first murder victim. Why would she keep that fact a secret if she wasn't involved in his murder? I consider myself a good judge of character, but what if I'm wrong? Lola's trip to Chicago certainly seemed unexpected. I wonder why she went.

"Asher and Mike have been sneaking around

Tyler's shop and doing research on him at the library, and we have evidence that Tyler, Frank, and Sam, were all in jail in Chicago at about the same time, and that Fergusson was a frequent visitor to the jail. Then there's Billy, a stranger in town who might have ties to Tyler's past life," rattled off Sheriff Houtman.

"What about the shady characters who frequent his shop? One of them could have a grudge against Tyler. Maybe the same person who murdered Bobby Jo Love murdered Tyler," said Sadie.

"That's a distinct possibility. We do think Tyler may have had a connection to Bobby Jo the victim found in the alley behind The Joker's Den. One of the victim's friends could think that Tyler murdered Bobby Jo, so they murdered Tyler to exact revenge for killing their friend. We will explore all possibilities, but right now, I need to question the two of you," said the determined inquisitor.

Sheriff Houtman took each of us into Sadie's office and questioned us, challenging any vague or unsure answers. Sadie mounted a vehement defense of Billy. She also told the sheriff they had gone to search the abandoned warehouses but had to return empty-handed because of Tyler's murder. She also reminded him about the scraps of sheet music. "You haven't done a single thing about finding Billy. You promised you would search for him. Now that there has been another murder, you need to find Billy fast before someone kills him instead of wasting time questioning Robin and me."

I was a fierce mother hen pecking at the enemy when Houtman asked questions about Asher and Mike. I also told Mark that he had left out one suspect, Mike's father, Sam, and informed the sheriff that we saw Sam huddled with Fergusson and Tyler at the library. I also reminded the sheriff that Sam and Frank were convicted felons who had done time together. Sam also often verbally abused his own child when Sam had too much to drink. In the movies, they always say, "Follow the money." Well, Lola found that money trail when she realized Ten Pins might be foreclosed on if Sam couldn't produce the back rent he owed."

Just as Houtman finished interviewing me, Mike and Asher entered Sweet Indulgences. "Mom, what happened? Sadie said something bad has happened, but she wouldn't tell us what. We just rushed back here and never got to search for Billy in the warehouses," said Asher. "What's going on?"

Turning to Sheriff Houtman, Asher continued, "Sheriff, we found out some interesting things about Fergusson and Tyler while we did our research that you might want to know."

"Fergusson isn't who he said he was," Mike said. "He has five missing years where we can't find any work history, no real estate transactions, and no other type of employment history. We suspect that he might have been in prison and possibly at the same time as my dad. Could he have known Tyler and Frank from prison also? Do you think he could be responsible for Billy's kidnapping or even for Bobby Jo Love's murder?"

The sheriff put up his hand. "Boys, stop talking right now. I've heard enough accusations. I'll do the investigating and the accusing. You all need to butt out."With that said, Mark Houtman turned to head out, back to his office while saying to Mike and Asher, "I'd like to interview you each about Mopey Tyler's death.

Don't leave this shop. I have some calls to make then I'll be back and will question each of you separately." Sheriff Houtman then fled before I could jump again into attack-mother mode.

"Whoa! What's Sheriff Houtman talking about? Tyler is dead? When, where, who?" the boys both blustered.

Sadie took charge. "Calm down, boys, calm down. Sit down at the table, and I'll fix you some hot chocolate, then we can tell you what we know."

Sadie busied herself with getting the comfort food for the boys just as Lola walked in.

"Ms. George, Sadie, why is there a huge crowd outside The Joker's Den? What's going on?" Lola looked scared.

"Lola, sit down here with the boys, and we'll fill you all in at once," I said in my motherly way. After all, Lola was like a daughter to me, and it upset me to see her so agitated, even though I was not as convinced of her innocence as I had been.

While Sadie and I told Lola and the boys what had transpired, Sheriff Houtman and Deputy Murphy headed to the abandoned warehouses to see what they could find. Much as the sheriff hated to admit that I was right, he knew they needed to rapidly find Billy in case he was in danger.

Chapter 44

The Warehouses

Both lawmen headed to the warehouse district. Sadie had given the sheriff the addresses of the abandoned warehouses so Deputy Murphy ran them through the database of properties in the warehouse district and discovered that Fergusson's Welcome Realty owned two of the properties.

Guns in hand, the two lawmen approached the first property. It was a dilapidated gray building with black shutters all askew and with a broken sign that said, "Delaney's Imports". Cautiously, they entered through a broken window on the side. Empty. Then they approached the second building. It was also in poor condition, and the back door was ajar. With guns drawn, they entered and climbed the steep stairs.

Just as Deputy Murphy reached the locked room, they heard Billy yell, "Don't come in here. I am armed and won't hesitate to kill you."

"Billy, it's Sheriff Houtman and Deputy Murphy. Stand back."

"Fergusson and Tyler locked me in here after they kidnapped me. Please, get me out of here."

"Hang on, Billy. We'll open this door."

Deputy Murphy went to his Jeep and took out a crowbar he always carried for emergencies. As he was retrieving the crowbar, Murphy spotted a suspicious character with a hoodie, and yelled, "Stop, police." The man kept on running, hopped inside his car, and sped away.

Deputy Murphy gave up the chase. "I really need to get in shape. I should have caught that guy," Murphy said as he described the runner to Houtman. "I didn't get a clear look at him as he ran away."

Houtman said, "Forget the runner now. We need to get this door unlocked."

Murphy leaned on the crowbar until the lock broke.

Billy rushed to the two lawmen. He tried to look brave, but Sheriff Houtman could see the boy was shaking and close to tears. The sheriff wasn't usually very sympathetic, but he knew how much Sadie liked Billy and decided to cut him some slack. He gave Billy a pat on the back and said, "Kid, that was clever of you, tearing up the sheet music. When your band friends spotted the musical notes on the ground, they were curious and pasted together all the scraps. They then recognized the music as part of the program the band is playing in the band competition. They were the ones that alerted Mike and Asher, then Ms. George and Sadie figured out where you were. We also suspected you were kidnapped because of the clue about homelessness. After contacting nearby homeless shelters, we found the one in Lennon where the director was panicked because a strange man, claiming to be Sadie's friend, hadn't returned you from lunch. When she described the stranger, he sounded a lot like Tyler so we showed her some pictures. She identified Tyler as the man."

The sheriff looked at the terrified kid. "Let's get

you some food before I interrogate you. I have a whole list of questions that need answering."

"Yes, sir," Billy said shakily. He was still scared and kept looking over his shoulder for Tyler or Fergusson. He was also worried that Sheriff Houtman would discover his secret. If the sheriff discovers he's an orphan, child welfare will be called, and they could send him away from his life in Pittman.

Sheriff Houtman and Deputy Murphy returned to Sweet Indulgences with Billy in tow. Robin, Sadie, Lola, and the boys were ecstatic and ran up to Billy, throwing questions at him. Sadie broke through the babbling people and pulled Billy into a tight hug.

"Hold it, everyone," the sheriff said. "I will be the first person to interrogate Billy, but after he has eaten. I don't want anyone saying a word about what has gone on here since his kidnapping. Enjoy the fact that he is safe, but silence is now mandatory. Robin, not a word. I mean it."

While the sheriff was issuing this ultimatum, Lola was behind his back mimicking the sheriff. She made weird faces and shook her finger at everyone. The others had to put their hands over their mouths to keep from laughing out loud.

Billy wolfed down the sandwiches and chips that Sadie prepared for him. He felt a little better, but he wasn't looking forward to the sheriff's questions.

Billy saw how sympathetically Sadie looked at him so he ignored the sheriff's silence mandate and began to talk. "I'm sorry I scared you all," Billy said. "Tyler and Fergusson told me that you, Ms. George, and Lola were trying to steal my inheritance from Aunt Dehlia and said they were trying to protect me. I couldn't believe their story. You all would never betray me. Plus, I had no idea Aunt Dehlia left me an inheritance, so how could you know about the inheritance?"

Sadie stood up abruptly and went to a drawer behind the display counter. She took out an envelope. "Billy, when you crashed on Robin's rug, we found this locket that had fallen out of your pocket. Do you recognize the picture in the locket?"

"Yes, yes. That's my Aunt Dehlia. She gave it to me after we visited a fair near my Grandpa Wood's farm. I remember how much fun we had that day. Aunt Dehlia did a reading of *Fire the Hiccupping Dragon* to a crowd of kids. They loved the story and ran around the fair hiccupping and laughing."

"Billy, there also was this key from your pocket. It looks like a safe deposit key. Do you know what it's for?" asked Sadie.

"I remember that Aunt Dehlia gave it to me when she left the farm to go to New York City. She said I should guard it because someday it would mean a lot to me, but she never told me what it opened. I was so upset that she was leaving I didn't ask why the key was so important."

Sheriff Houtman said, "I'll take the key. It looks like a safe deposit key. We'll track down what bank it's from and find out what your Aunt Dehlia wanted you to have."

Chapter 45

Interrogations

After Billy finished eating, Sheriff Houtman took him into Sadie's office at Sweet Indulgences and said, "Sit down, Billy, and listen. While you allege that you were kidnapped, there was a second murder. You know that you are one of the prime suspects in the murder of the band member, Bobby Jo Love. We checked to see if there was any connection between you and Bobby Jo Love. Did you kill Bobby Jo because you suspected him of selling drugs? Where did you meet him? Are you familiar with his Bluegrass band?"

"I told you I don't know Bobby Jo."

"Perhaps you confronted Bobby Join in anger and hit him with the band trophy that you got that day at the band banquet. This might not have been premeditated murder, but things just got out of control. What do you say about this?" demanded the sheriff.

Billy couldn't believe what the sheriff was saying so he just stared at him and didn't answer.

The sheriff continued, "You could have staged your kidnapping. It was convenient and clever to send the cryptic text to Mike and Asher. It seems strange that you would be poised and thoughtful enough to compose this while in the throes of being kidnapped. You also could have locked the door of the warehouse yourself.

We just took your word that it was locked from the outside when we busted in. You could have killed Tyler and then locked yourself in the warehouse, creating this elaborate kidnapping hoax."

Billy stared at the sheriff. "You can't believe that. What about Tyler kidnapping me from the homeless shelter?"

"Maybe you weren't kidnapped at all, but you convinced Tyler that you just wanted to go home, so he took you back to Pittman."

"Why would I do this? Why would I kill Tyler?" screamed Billy.

"Maybe Tyler had some connection to your dad or your mom?" accused the sheriff. "You keep telling everyone that your mom and dad are okay with your staying overnight at various houses, but no one has met your parents. Have they abandoned you? Have you run away from home? What do Bobby Jo or Tyler have to do with your parents? You need to start talking, young man."

Billy collapsed back into his chair as if all the wind had left his body. "Sheriff, you can't really believe this untrue, unbelievable fairytale. Your imagination has kidnapped your brain."

Billy was done talking to the accusing fool. Some adults just can't trust a kid. He refused to say another word.

Sheriff Houtman took Deputy Murphy aside to talk to him. Houtman was certain he was onto something. Billy had appeared out of nowhere when he crashed into Robin's store. His parents were nowhere to be found. No one knows where he was living prior to his taking up residence with Sadie.

The sheriff said to Deputy Murphy, "See what you can find out about this Grandpa Wood and Aunt Dehlia that Robin and Sadie were talking about. Maybe that will lead to the whereabouts of Billy's parents. Billy seems like a likable kid, but that could just be an act. He could be a con artist. Something is fishy about him, and until we find out what, he will remain my prime suspect for both murders, no matter what Sadie and Robin think."

Chapter 46

Lola Returns to Chicago

When Billy and the sheriff went into Sadie's office, Lola seemed lost in thought. Robin noticed her pale face, and determined expression, and asked, "Lola, what's wrong? Is something bothering you?"

"Robin, I need a couple of days off. I need to take care of some personal business in Chicago," said Lola.

"Well, of course, you can take some time off. I can take care of the store, and Asher can help me after school. Take as much time as you need, but, Lola, if you need anything or need to talk, you know you can trust me. Also, you should stay in town until Sheriff Houtman has questioned you."

Lola was no longer the nervous, anxious woman she had been when she first came to Pittman from California. The transformation had taken about a year, during which I showered her with as much motherly love as possible. I knew that something had happened when she was younger and living in Chicago, and I wasn't sure about her life in Hollywood because she seemed very reluctant to talk about her past.

Something serious must be troubling her. I hope it doesn't have anything to do with Mopey Tyler's murder, though she would have a motive because she knew he was dealing drugs, and Lola hates everything about the drug trade.

****

After Robin gave Lola permission to have a few days off, Lola left the Bookworm Shop. She checked the train schedule. Ignoring the warning not to leave town, she decided to risk taking the train from Pittman to New York, then on to Chicago's Union Station. She was on a mission to find some member of the Lovey Doves' Bluegrass Band. She had to find out from them if Tyler was the person who sold the drugs to her mom. She kept having nightmares about the day she received the phone call from the policeman:

"Ma'am, we found a woman unconscious, next to the fountain in Grant Park. Your number was in her wallet as a contact. Since you have the same last name, we presumed you were related to her."

"Yes, yes, that's my mom. Is she okay?"

"The rescue squad rushed her to the nearest hospital. I'll have an officer pick you up and take you there. That way, the officer can question you on the way. Please tell him everything you know about your mom's life with the Lovey Doves' Bluegrass Band. Give me your address, and someone will be right there."

Lola started to shake as she vividly remembered the nurse, meeting her at the emergency door and telling her that her mom didn't make it. Her mom had led a very troubled life. When she was high or drunk, she became either sullen and quiet, or violent and lashed out at Lola who, as she grew older, knew instinctively when to hide. Lola would grab her fluffy lamb, Lambchop, and run upstairs and hide behind her bed, hugging Lambchop tightly.

Lola would murmur over and over to herself, "Mom does love me. She does. She's just sick."

From the moment the nurse told Lola that her mom had OD'd on heroin, Lola vowed that she would never associate with anyone pushing drugs on innocent or weak people. She had met some of the scuzzy characters who plied members of the band with drugs, and she hated them. Tyler reminded her of those evil people whenever she ran into him.

Lola shook away the memories and headed straight home to pack and get to the next train. Chicago would always be a nightmare to her, and Lola was determined to emerge whole from this nightmare.

Chapter 47

Back to the Murder Board

After finishing Billy's interrogation, Sheriff Houtman wasn't sure he believed all that Billy had told him. If Billy was a con artist, he was a good liar. The sheriff wouldn't get much more out of Billy now since he absolutely refused to say another word. Since Sadie believed in Billy, Mark Houtman was willing to give Billy the benefit of the doubt until he questioned all the suspects and reexamined all the evidence.

He phoned Murphy and told him to meet him back at the station. They needed to narrow down the suspect pool. It was time to revisit the Murder Board.

Murphy arrived with black coffee and delicious sandwiches from Sweet Indulgences. As they ate, they stared at the Murder Board lost in thought because they now not only had the burglary and vandalism cases but also kidnapping and two murders to solve.

REVISED MURDER BOARD—CLUES, EVIDENCE, MOTIVES

1st first murder of Billy Jo Love

2nd murder of Mopey Tyler

FACTS:

1st Murder weapon is Mike's band trophy

Who had access to this trophy?

2nd Murder weapon was also a band trophy.

1st and 2nd Three sets of fingerprints on both trophies, Mike's, Sam's, and Billy's

2nd Another smudged print was found on Billy's trophy.

1st Time of death of Bobby Jo Love—sometime on Saturday night or Sunday morning according to the coroner's report.

2nd Time of Tyler's murder Monday night or early Tuesday morning.

MIKE

Alibi

1st Sam displayed all the band trophies at Ten Pins so anyone would have access to them.

Saturday—at band competition—Didn't get home until late.

Sunday morning?

2nd At band practice Monday evening

Went home to bed about 11:00 p.m.

No one saw him at home.

Searching for Billy on Tuesday morning with Sadie.

Opportunity

1st Seen at Joker's Den snooping around the day before Bobby Jo's murder.

Could he have been figuring out how and where to kill Tyler and mistakenly killed one of his customers?

2nd Can't account for the next week on Monday night or early Tuesday morning when Tyler was killed.

Says he was exhausted Monday after band practice and went to sleep.

Sam didn't see Mike at home on Monday, but Sam came in very late that night.

Mike went with Sadie to search for Billy early

Tuesday morning.

Motive

1st Hated how Tyler treated Robin and Sadie who had been so good to him.

Didn't like Tyler hanging around with his dad and encouraging Sam to start drinking again.

If he killed one of Tyler's customers, he could blame the murder on Tyler.

2nd Maybe he decided that since Tyler wasn't blamed for the first murder, he would go right to the source of his hatred and kill Tyler.

BILLY

Alibi

1st Missing because he says he was kidnapped.

2nd We only have Billy's word that he was kidnapped though he put on a pretty convincing act when sheriff found him in the warehouse.

Opportunity

1st He did have time to plan a murder.

2nd Only had an opportunity if he faked his kidnapping.

His fingerprints were on both murder weapons.

Motive

Hated Tyler because of his treatment of Sadie and because he was a drug dealer.

Revenge—Tyler or Bobby Jo—connection to Billy's dad's death?

LOLA

Alibi

?????—Need to question her

Opportunity

???????

Young and strong.

Could easily overpower both victims.

Motive

Revenge—Tyler ogles her and treats her with disrespect.

Dad and Mom died of a drug overdose.

Tyler or Bobby Jo might have sold drugs to her mom's band members

ASHER

Alibi

?????—Need to question him.

Opportunity

?????—Need to question him

Motive

1st Tyler hates Asher's mom.

May want to ruin Tyler's business because Tyler might have had Bobby Jo sell drugs to some of Asher's fellow band members.

2nd Maybe he decided to go straight to the source and kill Tyler.

ROBIN

Alibi

??????

Opportunity

?????—Her shop wasn't vandalized. Could she be the vandal if not the murderer?

Motive

Recently witnessed Robin's temper.

1st She has been researching Tyler.

Maybe Tyler had attacked Billy, Asher, or Mike or tried to sell them drugs.

2nd Maybe in a fit of anger, she attacked Tyler and meant to kill him, or it was an accident.

She seems to be the least likely suspect.

SADIE

Alibi

1st Why would Sadie vandalize her own shop?

2nd Went to warehouses Tuesday morning.

No alibi for Monday night.

Opportunity

Has skills she learned to protect her family from ISIS.

Owns a gun to protect herself who might hunt her down, but the murder weapon wasn't a gun.

Motive

1st Could Bobby Jo be a member of ISIS here in Pittman to track down Sadie?

2nd Hates Tyler because of his prejudice and horrid treatment of her.

Publicly yelled at him in anger.

Tyler intimidates and threatens her just like ISIS members did in Lebanon.

Please don't let it be Sadie.

FERGUSSON

Alibi

???????—Need to question.

Opportunity

1st No one would question his appearance in the alley because he owned many of the shops.

2nd Tyler and he were constantly together so he knew Tyler's schedule.

Had many opportunities to ruin Tyler. Why now?

Had a key to The Joker's Den.

Motive

Money!!!!!

Needed property on Farley Square for a condo development.

Bank records show that Fergusson and Tyler are linked financially.

Why a 5-year gap in Fergusson's history?

Did he know Tyler during that time??

Did he know Bobby Jo?

SAM

Must question him soon.

Alibi

1st Ten Pins closes at 11:00 p.m.

Was Sam or Frank working at the Bowling Alley the night of the murder?

All depends on time of murder.

2nd If Tyler was killed Monday night, Sam could kill after he left work.

Need to question Frank about timing.

Opportunity

1st Had access to murder weapon.

Seen conferring with Fergusson and Tyler.

2nd Had access to trophies.

Was he involved with the supposed kidnapping?

Was he the person that Murphy spotted running away?

Motive

Money

1st In debt—Desperately needed money.

Maybe being blackmailed because of violating parole.

2nd Payoff as a hit man would be lucrative.

FRANK

Alibi

1st& 2nd Was covering the bar for Sam.

Opportunity

Not guilty of kidnapping since Billy didn't identify

him.

Check if anyone besides Sam can verify his alibi.

Motive

If he was in prison with Tyler, could hold a grudge for something that happened in prison.

1st Loyalty to Sam.

2nd Overall everyone liked Frank so why would he kill Billy Joe? Any connection to the Blue Grass Band?

DRUG CUSTOMER

Alibi

Unknown ??????

Seems far-fetched since no one can identify any of the strange customers.

Opportunity

Many unsavory characters had been seen shopping at The Joker's' Den and could return unnoticed when it got dark.

Motive

1st Wrong time, wrong place?

2nd Maybe Tyler refused to sell this person drugs.

Maybe Tyler jacked up the price of drugs so the victim went after Tyler in anger.

Someone from his past returning for revenge.

****

Deputy Murphy filled Houtman in on Aunt Dehlia's story and told him he found out that Billy stayed on Grandpa Wood's farm for several summers. After this review, Deputy Murphy and Sheriff Houtman decided to question the rest of the suspects. Murphy went to Sweet Indulgences to question Asher and Mike while Houtman called and left messages for Sam and Fergusson to meet him within the hour at the police station. While waiting for them, Houtman called Lola and asked her also to come in for questioning. When she didn't answer, he called me to see if I knew where Lola was. He was quite upset to learn that Lola had taken time off, and that I knew about it.

"You let her go? Doesn't Lola realize she is a prime suspect in the murders? What were you thinking?"

"Just calm down," I shouted into the phone at the ever-accusing sheriff. "Lola didn't kill anyone. If you knew her at all, you would realize that she was traumatized by the death of her mother and would never commit murder herself."

"What time did she leave? Was she going to Chicago or California? What's her destination?"

Shaking from anger, I answered, "I'm not exactly sure what time she left. She just asked for some time off and didn't share any details with me. I think she left about an hour ago. I don't know when she left town. She was driving, taking the bus, flying, taking the train, or just getting on her magic carpet—I have no clue. I don't know for sure that her destination is Chicago, though I think she mentioned the city. Lola has been upset, and I didn't want to ask her why. I respect her privacy. I also told her not to leave town because she needed to be questioned by you, and she assured me she would answer any questions you have for her. I had no reason to doubt her."

Because Lola had only asked for a few days off, Houtman guessed she headed to Chicago rather than California. Houtman alerted all the agencies involved from Massachusetts to Illinois. He told all the transportation centers to be on the lookout for a person wanted for questioning in a murder and sent out a picture and description of Lola to all authorities, including those in Los Angeles, just in case.

Chapter 48

Fergusson Finalizes the Paperwork

After Tyler's murder was discovered Tuesday morning, Fergusson went to the lawyer's office and played the tape of fake Billy swearing that he had a disability that would not allow him to meet with strange men. Mr. Wright believed Fergusson and gave him the financial guardianship papers he would need to handle Dehlia's inheritance for Billy.

Fergusson then went to Welcome Realty and forged Billy's signature on the papers. He then immediately went to the bank and made all the money transfers from Billy's inheritance from Aunt Dehlia. He split the money between his business account and his personal account. He told the banker he would have Billy set up an account in his own name in the near future as soon as he could convince Billy to accompany him to the bank.

"If I can't convince Billy to come into the bank, is it possible to just give me a form for him to sign, and I'll cosign on the account since I'm legally his financial guardian?" With Tyler dead, Fergusson was now Billy's sole guardian and responsible for managing Billy's inheritance from Dehlia.

Fergusson needed to make the transfers before his lawyer or the manager at the bank spoke to Billy or the sheriff. Fergusson also made himself scarce to escape the sheriff's interrogation.

Fergusson set up his alibi for Tyler's murder by leaving voice messages for Sadie and Robin that he needed to leave town last night to go to Chicago to shore up one of his major real estate deals. He told us it would take him a few weeks to solve these problems, but since he couldn't reach the sheriff, he gave them a fake phone number in case Houtman needed to contact him.

Chapter 49

Sam Refuses to Go Back to Jail

Tuesday afternoon, Sam called in Frank, gave him a stack of money, and asked him to run Ten Pins until he returned. Also, he asked him to tell anyone who asked that he had left town last week and should return in a couple of weeks. "I don't want anyone thinking I had anything to do with either of these murders," Sam firmly stated.

Though puzzled as to why anyone would suspect Sam was involved, Frank was loyal to Sam no matter what, so he put the money away. "Sam, be careful. I'm not sure what you have gotten yourself into, and I don't want to know, but don't risk going back to prison for anyone or anything. We left that life behind and must not return. You know that I've got your back. Take care."

This alibi he'd created would let Sam off the hook for the murders and the kidnapping. He gave Frank the phone number of his new burner phone but told him not to share the number with anyone, not even Mike. If anyone asked or tried to reach him on his former cell, it would just show that the service has been discontinued. He also would call Mike and tell him he had to go out of town on business, and if he needs anything, to contact Frank for help.

Sam planned to hide all the payments from Fergusson in a new account he would open when he arrived in Chicago. He still had a few reputable and reliable friends there from his past life, so he planned to hang out with them. No one would guess his whereabouts.

Sam packed his bags, loaded up his truck, and left before the sheriff or Deputy Murphy could question him.

Since Fergusson knew how Sam had tried to cut Tyler out of his share of the real estate deals, Sam was sure Fergusson would not only blame Billy's kidnapping on him but would also accuse Sam of murdering Tyler to get Tyler's share of the real estate commissions. Sam was petrified that the stupid sheriff might believe him.

Chapter 50

Lola Confronts Her Demons

Lola left Tuesday night for Chicago. Wednesday morning, once she disembarked from the train, she headed right to the area around Northwestern University and walked down by the lake. As she crossed the bridge over the stream flowing on campus from Lake Michigan, she stopped and stared at the giant catfish under the bridge. The whiskers on the catfish reminded Lola of her dad's scraggly beard. How she had loved her dad. He was the only one who cared for her when she was small. How dare he die. If he had taken care of himself, and quit drinking, smoking pot, and using hard drugs, he would be still alive, and her life would be so different.

After his death, Lola used to come down by the lake and walk for hours to avoid going home to her abusive mother. When she reached Clark Street, she would leave Lake Michigan and cut up to the Lincoln Park Zoo. This inner-city zoo, founded in 1868, had a special meaning to her. She now stood under the weeping willow outside the zoo's entrance. Lola entered and headed right for the gorilla display. Many times, her dad had stood with Lola, mimicking the gorillas. She laughed as she pictured the faces he made and the contortions he went through as he imitated the smallest gorillas.

Lola remembered the store on Clark Street where her dad bought his liquor and drugs on the way home from their weekly excursions to the zoo. If anyone remembered her dad, it would be one of the clerks in the store. Lola set out on her quest for answers.

When she approached Baines' Tobacco Shop, Lola timidly entered. She approached a friendly-looking young fellow. "Sir, I wonder if you can help me? Many years ago, when this store was called The Den of Thieves, my dad used to shop here every week. I wonder if there is anyone here who would remember that time and maybe remember my dad?"

"I don't know anyone who worked here then, but I do know a little of the shop's history.

"About eight years ago, a man named Tyler opened The Den of Thieves as a corner tobacco and food shop. He sold convenience foods, cigars and cigarettes, and was licensed to sell liquor. What he wasn't licensed for was to sell drugs and launder money. Two years after he opened, the police raided his store and sent him off to jail after a contentious trial. That's when Mr. Donnelly, a real estate magnate, stepped in and bought the shop."

He continued, "The only problem with that deal was that Mr. Donnelly was also a shady character. Two months after opening, the police again raided The Den of Thieves and found other illegal transactions taking place. Loans for real estate transactions were obtained fraudulently, promises were not fulfilled, corners were cut, and buyers found fault with sloppy record keeping. Donnelly was arrested for fraud, made bail, and managed to disappear. He was never found to be brought to trial.

"Mr. Donnelly was quite rich and everyone was sure he'd change his identity and resurface somewhere, in another country. Wherever he relocated, it would have to have snow because he was an avid skier. I'm sorry I can't be of any more help with finding your dad, Miss."

"Thank you. You've given me some very helpful information," said Lola as she exited the shop.

Lola knew she needed to get this information to Robin, Sadie, and Sheriff Houtman. If Fergusson is Mr. Donnelly, and he bought The Den of Thieves from Tyler, that would explain how they knew each other. But before contacting anyone, Lola needed to track down someone from her mom's band, Lovey Dove's Bluegrass Band. She took the L to the Lawrence Avenue stop and then walked to a park on Damen Avenue where many impromptu concerts took place each afternoon. Lola was hoping to meet up with one of her mom's former band members.

An article search in the *Chicago Tribune* had turned up a mention of Emma Mae Fredericks who played guitar with the Lovey Doves. The article said she now played solo concerts in the parks and sometimes hooked up with local bands for park concerts. Lola hoped to find Emma Mae, who she remembered was one of her mother's friends. She was pretty sure Emma Mae could point her to the supplier of the drugs that killed her mom and dad.

When Lola reached Damen Avenue, she crossed the street and followed the music she heard emerging from the center of the park. The band was playing a catchy tune. As she waited for them to finish, she kept looking around, having this feeling as though being watched.

Spotting Lola watching the band, a policewoman approached her and quickly snapped handcuffs on her. Lola screamed. The band stopped playing. Emma Mae jumped off the stage, recognizing her, and ran toward her, yelling and screaming at the policewoman.

Sergeant Bob Wagner stepped into this chaos and said to Emma Mae, "Miss, calm down, or I will cuff you and take you down to the station." Sergeant Wagner turned to Lola, struggling with the policewoman, and yelled, "Stop this caterwauling immediately."

Surprised, Lola froze and then began to cry. Huge sobs erupted.

"Take her to my squad car. I'll sort this out," said Officer Wagner.

The policewoman pushed Lola to the car and forced her into the back seat.

Emma followed Lola to the police car and through the window asked Lola why she was there. Lola sobbed, "I just needed to find out if you know who sold my mom the drugs that killed her."

Sergeant Wagner interrupted them, got into the car, and left for the station with Lola.

Emma Mae asked the policewoman where the sergeant was taking Lola. Emma Mae then hailed a taxi and headed to the station determined to help her friend's daughter.

Chapter 51

The Phone Call

Sadie, the boys, and I were waiting at Sadie's house for Sheriff Houtman and Deputy Murphy to update us on the progress of their investigation. Sadie kept looking over her shoulder whenever she went out. She was so afraid that one of the ISIS members from her village had tracked her down. When we heard through the grapevine that Sheriff Houtman was close to arresting a suspect for the two murders, we were anxious to hear who they had pegged as murderers. Since my opinion of the sheriff wasn't as positive as Sadie's, I didn't have a lot of hope that the bumbling fool would get it right, but, always a pragmatist, I was willing to wait and see.

Sadie had made her comfort food, eggplant and sauce, a dish with a name I can't pronounce. As everyone was spooning the sauce mixture on their rice, the sheriff and deputy came in.

Sadie said, "Sheriff, since you always seem to arrive at dinnertime, you might as well join us. You and Deputy Murphy can eat and talk at the same time as you fill us in on your findings."

Filling his plate with a generous helping of Sadie's concoction, the sheriff began to fill in our missing information. "First of all, we managed to link Mopey

Tyler to the break-ins and vandalism. His fingerprints were on the door handles to Klette's Pharmacy, and we found the missing prescription drugs in his back room. We also suspect that he was responsible for trashing Sweet Indulgences because we found the marker that was used to write the vile messages on Sadie's walls. It was hidden in the back of a drawer in The Joker's Den stockroom."

"That evil man. At least it wasn't an ISIS member as I feared." Sadie let out a breath of relief.

"But, Sheriff," I said, "why would Tyler vandalize his store?"

"We think Tyler wanted to throw suspicion off himself, and we guess that he needed the insurance money that would cover the damage. When we went over his books, it appeared Tyler owed loads of money to a lot of people."

"Does that mean that Asher, Mike, and Billy are off your suspect list?"

"For the vandalism, yes, but Lola is another story. She may have teamed up with Tyler. She's such a good little actress, and that may explain her disappearance."

"No, Sheriff, I can't believe Lola would team up with such an evil man. She also wouldn't help anyone who sells drugs. She hates everyone and everything that has to do with drugs because her mom and dad both died due to drug use."

"You're right about Lola hating drugs, Robin, but that very hatred gives Lola the perfect motive for killing Tyler and even for killing Bobby Jo Love, whom we suspect was either a drug seller or a drug user and connected to the band where Lola's mother sang."

The darn sheriff had me there. His case against

Lola was building, and I couldn't dispute any of it. I tried one more time to redeem Lola. "Sheriff, I just can't believe that a lovely, kind, loyal woman such as Lola could be a cold-hearted killer. She loves children and loves all of us. Surely, you can find another suspect. I'm sure when she returns, she will have a perfectly good reason to refute your charges."

"You mean *if* she returns. So far, no one can find her. Where is she? I have police in four states looking for her."

Just then the phone rang. Asher jumped up to get it. Billy looked so scared that I started to worry he had a connection to Tyler that I didn't know about. *Could Billy have been hired by Tyler to trash the stores? He certainly needed money. Could he have been hired to kill Bobby Jo? Tyler probably paid well for someone to commit a crime.*

"Wow, Mom," Asher yelled. "It's a call from someone at the Chicago City police department calling collect for you."

I raced to the phone. "Yes, yes, put her on."

Sheriff Houtman's phone also rang. "You have. Great. I'll send a deputy to your jail to extradite her and bring her back to Pittman. Thanks for your quick work."

Mark Houtman put his phone down and announced to all that Lola was in the custody of the Chicago police, and Deputy Murphy would take the train to Chicago, pick her up and bring her back to Pittman.

"That was Lola," I told everyone. "She was sobbing and said that she had nothing to do with Bobby Jo's death, and when the Chicago police accused her of murdering Tyler, she broke down right in front of them.

She begged me to tell Sheriff Houtman she was innocent and would never kill anyone."

"As soon as I get home, I'll explain why I left Pittman and came to Chicago. Please tell everyone to have faith in my innocence," Lola begged.

Sheriff Houtman listened to my account of my phone call and said, "I don't believe Lola's story. She had motive and opportunity for both murders. Robin, you are so influenced by a sob story that you can't face reality."

With that statement, the sheriff and deputy left to prepare to pick up Lola and then charge her when she arrived in Pittman.

I felt so sorry for Lola, and I could understand why Sheriff Houtman thought she was his prime suspect, but I just can't believe Lola would kill someone. Which leads me to the dilemma of if not Lola, who else could have killed Tyler? Could it have been Sam? Where is Sam? I wonder if he can at least provide an alibi for the time of each murder. Sam is desperate to get money for his bowling alley. Could he have known Bobby Jo from when he lived in Chicago? Maybe Sam knew Tyler from his time in prison. Tyler could have paid Sam to kill Bobby Jo, and then Tyler could have blackmailed Sam, and that would give Sam a motive for killing Tyler.

I pulled Sadie aside and said to her, "The sheriff is jumping to conclusions. There are other credible suspects who are more guilty than Lola. Maybe we need to put our heads together and come up with a list of suspects other than just Lola. We need to convince the sheriff to investigate the others. His first reaction to our suggestions is bound to be dismissal since he thinks we meddle far too much in his business."

Chapter 52

Billy Confesses All

"I can't stand this lack of trust from everyone," Sadie said. "I find myself looking over my shoulder all the time. Sheriff Houtman is accusing good people of murder. I tried to talk to him today and tell him he was looking at the wrong people. He wouldn't listen to me. I told him how evil the ISIS followers were and explained that what he was missing was the element of evil. Lola isn't evil. Sam, though a convicted felon and a sometimes-negligent father, would never kill anyone unless provoked. I was even suspecting the bartender, good, kind Frank, only because he loves Bluegrass music and the first victim was connected to a Bluegrass band. Robin, somehow, we must get through to that stubborn man. He's driving me crazy with his one-track mind."

Sadie wiped her eyes and continued. "Do you think Sam is drinking again and could have committed these terrible murders and been involved with Billy's kidnapping? Maybe Frank is involved because he's trying to cover for his friend? Could Mark Houtman be correct in his suspicions?"

"I don't know, Sadie, but I do know that the only evil person I know on Farley Square, besides Thomas Tyler, is Fergusson. Billy has identified both Tyler and

Fergusson as the kidnappers, though the sheriff hasn't yet arrested Fergusson. He's been sidetracked searching for Tyler's killer. He seems to have a hard time focusing on more than one thing at a time. By the way, has anyone seen Fergusson recently? Has the sheriff even interrogated him about the kidnapping and murders?"

Asher interrupted our discussion. "Hey, Mom, what do you think will happen to The Joker's Den now that Tyler is dead? Who owns it? Does Tyler have any relatives who would inherit his store?" The boys were eating ice cream sundaes. Comfort food seemed necessary to all of them at the moment. "You didn't find evidence of any relatives when you researched his past, did you?"

"No, but we didn't even know his name was Thomas. I guess you'll have to ask the sheriff who inherits. Why do you want to know?"

"Well," said Asher, "all of us boys had this idea awhile ago for a bike shop to open on Farley Square instead of The Joker's Den. Our friend, Wayne, who graduated two years ago, wants to buy a building and open a retail bike store and a repair shop for bikes and motorcycles. Billy was hoping to work there."

"Billy, that brings me back to your family history," said Robin. "You lied to us about your parents. In all this chaos about the kidnapping, no parents have shown up to inquire about you. How do you explain that? Also, your Aunt Dehlia lived with you when you were younger. Where did you live, and who did you live with? You owe us some answers, young man."

Billy looked down at the ground and stayed silent.

"Don't give us the silent routine. Don't lie to us

again. We care about you, and that's why we're asking," said an angry Sadie. "I've taken you into my home, and we all have defended you to the sheriff. Now, be brave and tell us your story."

Sadie stood glaring at Billy and refused to back down. Her Lebanese temper was flaring.

Billy looked up at Sadie. He contritely told everyone his tale of growing up with a mother who abandoned him at his grandfather's farm, where Aunt Dehlia also lived. "I'm sorry I deceived you, but I was afraid of being sent to an orphanage. I'm quite capable of living on my own and refuse to go the foster home or orphanage route. If I told any of you about my grandparents' death and the unknown whereabouts of my mom and Aunt Dehlia, you would be obliged to inform the authorities, and I would have to run away again. Here, I have friends and the band to support me, and I can get odd jobs to support myself. I appreciate you taking me in, but I just couldn't put you in the position of lying about me or turning me in to the sheriff. Please don't hate me."

Sadie walked over to Billy and put her arms around him. "Billy, you're part of our family now. We'll work out something, but we do have to inform the sheriff. He has a kind side, and I think I can persuade him to let you stay with me or Robin. Don't worry. I'm a persuasive lady when I put my mind to it."

He looked up at her. "I really appreciate your offer to let me live with you. Maybe this inheritance from Aunt Dehlia that the kidnappers were after is a gift that will give me a means of support. I just need a chance to prove myself."

"Billy, what about that key that dropped out of

your pocket?"

"My Aunt Dehlia gave me the locket with my mom's picture and gave me a key to what Dehlia said would make me and all children happy. She told me to hide the key until I needed it. She also said that Mr. Brinkman at the Lee Bank and Loan Company near my grandpa's farm would explain everything to me when the time comes."

"Billy, we need to go to that bank and find out what this key reveals. After we get it back from Sheriff Houtman, we are going on a road trip."

Chapter 53

Face the Consequences

Frank frantically called Sam and urged him to return home because the sheriff wanted to question him about Tyler's murder. Houtman was suspicious that Sam or maybe even Frank killed Tyler. "I can't lie for you anymore. I don't intend to go to jail again for anybody. If I must, I'll leave town and disappear."

Sam said, "Calm down, Frank, neither of us is going back to jail. The sheriff is wrong. I didn't kill Tyler and obviously, neither did you. I'll come home this afternoon and get everything straightened out."

Frank didn't feel any better after talking to Sam. He should follow his own advice and leave town immediately. Frank had kept an emergency bag filled with a week's necessities ever since he got out of prison. He also helped himself to extra cash from the register each week to build up a reserve fund just in case of an emergency, or if he had a falling out with Sam.

****

Lola returned from Chicago about four o'clock, and Deputy Murphy promptly whisked her off to jail without allowing her to talk to me or Sadie. Though Sheriff Houtman had yet to track down Fergusson, he decided to call together the suspects and anyone connected to them. We were all to meet at six at the jail. If he didn't have a definitive suspect by then, he would play the Columbo game of gathering all the suspects together and making someone identify the murderer or confess.

Promptly at six, Sadie and I, with the three boys in tow, arrived at the jail. Deputy Murphy had us all sit in a circle, and then the sheriff entered with Lola. She looked exhausted and wouldn't even look at any of us. Just as we were seated, Sam and Frank entered and sat with us.

"Does anyone know whether Fergusson got my message to meet here?" asked Sheriff Houtman.

"I haven't seen him since yesterday." I looked at the others. They were all shaking their heads.

"Where did you see him, and what time was it?" asked the sheriff.

"Well, it was after lunch because I was just coming back from Sweet Indulgences, and I saw Fergusson coming out of the bank."

"Did he have anything with him?

"A folder and a black briefcase, I think."

"Has anyone seen Fergusson since noon yesterday?" asked the sheriff. No one had. "I tried his mobile phone and his office phone, and they go right to voice mail."

Lola chimed in. "He also has a burner phone that I would call him on when I was going to meet one of his clients that he expected me to take to dinner and do other things with. I have the number."

Lola gave the sheriff the number. When he called, Fergusson answered. "Why, I'm so sorry, Sheriff. I didn't get your message about the meeting. I've been feeling quite sick since yesterday afternoon so I came home and crawled into bed and haven't been answering the phone or the doorbell. I keep this emergency phone by my bed in case anyone needs me right away. I can come to the meeting in about a half hour if you want, but I would hate to expose everyone to what I have. I think it's the flu."

Gullible Sheriff Houtman was relieved Fergusson hadn't left town and that he had a valid reason for not answering the summons. I was suspicious of this excuse. He didn't look very sick when I saw him at noon yesterday as he was skipping down the bank steps.

"Well, I'll deal with Fergusson later. He has the flu and doesn't want to expose all of us. Right now, I want answers. We now know that Tyler is the one who murdered Bobby Jo. Tyler needed to silence Bobby Jo because he was using blackmail to threaten Tyler. He said that he would reveal Tyler's prison time served for drug dealing in Chicago and the fact that Tyler had sold drugs to the Lovey Doves' Bluegrass Band members. Evidence confirms Tyler's fingerprint was the one that was smeared on the first band trophy. We also have the word of a couple of merchants on Farley Lane that they saw lights on in The Joker's Den the night of the murder. We also know about his bragging to Frank about the killing. Billy has identified Tyler as one of his kidnappers if Billy's supposed kidnapping story holds up."

"Now, wait just a minute, Mark," Sadie burst in, "what do you mean 'supposed kidnapping'? We know Billy was kidnapped. We have his word, the note with the clues he sent, and we found the torn-up band music he left as a trail. You and Deputy Murphy found him locked in the warehouse and rescued him."

"Stop right there, Sadie. The way this interrogation is going to work is that I ask the questions. You all answer the questions, and nobody interrupts. I'll give you each a chance to respond to the question and answers given, but no interruptions, or I will have Deputy Murphy remove you from the room. Is that clear?" He glared at us.

"Lola, we'll start with you since you're the one that ran away when I wanted to question you. You had motive and opportunity to kill Tyler. Did you discover that Tyler was the one who sold drugs to your mom and dad and the Lovey Doves?"

"Yes, I recognized Bobby Jo from my mom's band. The day he came to Pittman, he called me and asked if I would join him for coffee to talk about my mom. I met him in Lennon and had coffee with him. He then told me about his plan to blackmail Tyler because Tyler had been the drug supplier for members of the band. I told him he was foolish to mess around with Tyler because he was a mean, vindictive man. Bobby Jo refused to listen. I was so angry. I wasn't sure whether Bobby Jo told me the truth about my mother, so that's when I decided to go to Chicago and find my mom's friend Emma Mae and ask her if it was true. If it was, I was going to inform the parole board and Sheriff Houtman. I had no idea that Tyler would stoop to murder. After Bobby Jo's murder, I decided to go to Chicago anyway and verify what Bobby Jo had told me. I also had no part in Tyler's murder since I wasn't even in town when he was killed."

"What time did you leave for Chicago? Did you drive or fly?"

"I left Tuesday about 8:00 p.m. I took the train, and your Deputy Murphy just now brought me back to town. I couldn't be in two places at once. When was Tyler killed?"

"I'll ask the questions," the Sheriff restated. "You could have hired someone to kill him using your trip as an alibi."

"And where would I get enough money to hire a killer, and where would I find such a person? I'm clearly not rich, and I don't exactly run around with a criminal crowd."

The sheriff was clearly getting frustrated. He hadn't expected such hostility on everyone's part. He thought the people in this room, other than the killer, would be glad he was getting to the bottom of all this.

Sheriff Houtman turned to Billy. "Okay. Sadie has vehemently defended you, but I'm not sure that you are so innocent. Why did you go to Lennon to the homeless shelter?"

"Someone in a ski mask had tried to kidnap me out on the street after band practice and botched the job. I was terrified. I needed to get away and consider who and why someone would want to kidnap me. I needed to get out of Pittman. I hitchhiked to Lennon, and while walking around town, I saw the sign for the Homeless Shelter and decided to hide out there until I figured out what to do, and why this was happening."

"In checking with the Homeless Shelter, we found out the first victim, Bobby Jo Love, had been at the homeless shelter for several weeks before his death. Did you meet him there?"

"What? No? I didn't even know him."

"Are you sure the two of you didn't plan the

blackmail of Tyler while you were there? You needed money, and Bobby Jo had a plan to get that money."

"I swear. I never met Bobby Jo."

"Humph, so you say. It seems suspicious to me. You also say that you were kidnapped during the time Tyler was killed, but you could have made up the story of the botched kidnapping since there are no witnesses. You could have composed the note to Asher hoping to provide an alibi. You could have locked yourself in and just told us the door was locked on the outside. We believed you that it was locked and bashed in the door. You could have locked it yourself from inside. Do you have any proof of your actual kidnapping?"

Billy thought fast. This was ridiculous. Surely, the Sheriff wasn't dense enough to believe this invented story. "I do have proof," Billy yelled out, frustrated. "Fergusson had papers drawn up for me to sign. I told him I needed time to think, and he said he would return that night. That's why I was so freaked out when you and Deputy Murphy came into the warehouse. I thought it was Fergusson returning. Find the lawyer who drew up the papers to give Tyler and Fergusson the right to act as my guardians over my Aunt Dehlia's bequest to me. Find that lawyer and those papers, and they will have dates on them that will show I was being held captive at the time of Tyler's death."

Chapter 54

The Sheriff's Inquiry

We tried to reach Fergusson on his emergency phone to ask about the lawyer and the papers Billy said he signed, but he wasn't answering. While Deputy Murphy set out to Fergusson's house to try and get answers, Sheriff Houtman told us to chill until Murphy arrived. We were fuming, plus we were starving. Sadie told the boys to go to Sweet Indulgences and get sandwiches and quarts of ice cream. We needed something to soothe our nerves. The sheriff, meanwhile, went back to his office to think. He knew he was close to finding enough evidence to charge someone with Tyler's murder, but who would he charge?

The door opened, and Deputy Murphy returned empty-handed. "I couldn't find Fergusson. No answer at his house, and the blinds are closed. I questioned the neighbors, but no one has seen him."

"I called him on a burner phone, and he said he was in bed with the flu, but why didn't he answer if he was home in his bed when you went to check on him?"

"His back door was open so I went in his house to check. Empty bed. Closets were empty. Computer was gone, and several file drawers were empty. No Fergusson. I stopped at his realty office and the same thing. Completely gone. File drawers empty," said Deputy Murphy.

"Look up Fergusson's license plate number and send out that number with a picture of Fergusson and a description of his car to all state police and local police from the surrounding towns. Also, alert the airports as far away as New York. He also, according to Lola, goes under the name, Donnelly. Search for both names. If he is trying to flee, we must find him. I'm guessing he's our most likely suspect for Tyler's murder. He's greedy, and he's been in cahoots with Tyler on various schemes that are illegal, including Billy's kidnapping. Maybe his greed got the best of him, and he decided to murder Tyler and cut him out as his partner and keep the money for himself. Check with the bank and see how much Fergusson withdrew and if he transferred any money to a different town or state. Also, check whether he transferred any money from Aunt Dehlia's gift to Billy. Meanwhile, I'm going to question Sam and then Frank."

When the Sheriff questioned Sam, he admitted to being an accessory in Billy's kidnapping, but he swore that Tyler and Fergusson threatened to harm Mike if Sam didn't participate in the kidnapping. He denied any connection to Bobby Jo's murder or Tyler's murder. The sheriff wanted to believe Sam, but something seemed off.

"Sheriff, you might want to examine Tyler's connections to Bobby Jo and his band," Sam said. "Tyler got drunk last week and was bragging about how he would never allow a punk like Bobby Jo to blackmail him. He also said that the kid got what he had coming to him. Frank and I both witnessed this threat to

Bobby Jo. Maybe Tyler killed the kid because Bobby Jo tried to blackmail Tyler by threatening to tell you that Tyler was a drug dealer."

The sheriff walked away after Sam left and consulted with Deputy Murphy. "I pretended that this was the first we were hearing about Tyler's involvement in Bobby Jo's death. Sam thinks Tyler killed Bobby Jo because of the blackmail. He doesn't realize how right he is. Billy told us about Tyler's partnership with Fergusson in the kidnapping, and Lola told us about the blackmail scheme. Do you think Fergusson decided to shut Tyler up about the kidnapping by killing him? With Tyler dead, Fergusson can blame him for everything, the vandalism, murder of Bobby Jo, and the kidnapping. That would leave Fergusson stock free of blame, particularly if he can throw the blame for Tyler's killing on Sam."

"It's suspicious that we can't seem to find Fergusson anywhere," said Murphy. "If he really is innocent, why has he disappeared?"

"Okay, let's question Frank. He was very forthcoming when he recognized the picture in the paper, so I'm sure he will be upfront with us about anything he knows. It's amazing how people tend to vent and tell their problems to a bartender. Then let's go back to our circle and see what the local sleuths have turned up regarding Tyler's murder. I've left them alone long enough for them to invent several scenarios, none of which I bet are true."

Frank seemed nervous when the sheriff began questioning him, but he proved to be a treasure trove of information when questioned. The sheriff felt confident he had enough evidence to solve the robbery and vandalism cases once he made one stop before going to Sweet Indulgences.

Chapter 55

Who Killed Tyler?

While Frank waited for Deputy Murphy to question him about Tyler's murder, he mulled over the present and past events.

Manning the bowling alley for Sam one afternoon, Frank looked lovingly at the photo of his wife and small son he carried in his wallet every day. He remembered when the police arrested him for armed robbery and tore him from his family.

His wife Mary sent monthly photos of Bobby growing up. His favorite pictures were Bobby's graduation picture and one of his first performances on stage playing his trusty guitar.

Frank's one regret was that when he was released from prison, Mary had no interest in reuniting their family. She had moved on now that Bobby was out on his own. Frank hoped to at least salvage some semblance of a relationship with his son. He had been tracking the band's schedule of concerts and hoped to meet with Bobby when his band passed through the Berkshires on tour.

Those pictures of his boy helped Frank through the tough years when he was imprisoned in Chicago. Frank met Sam three years into his sentence, and they became fast friends. Between Mary's letters, Sam's friendship, and the pictures of his child, Frank made it through his sentence. He vowed that he would never be locked up again.

He even dreamed of reuniting with his son. He saw that the Lovey Doves' Bluegrass Band was scheduled to perform at a festival this month in Pittman. He planned to confront Bobby, pour out his regret at being an absent parent, and beg his son to forgive him.

Before meeting with Bobby, Frank needed to deal with a problem. Frank knew Sam was drinking again, and that was dangerous. Sam was a mean drunk, and hung around with those two unsavory men, Fergusson and Tyler. Frank feared their unwelcome influence was putting Sam on another path to destruction and might get him involved. He can't violate his patrol and go back to prison. A reunion with his son was of paramount importance to him.

When Sam came into Ten Pins the Sunday night after the victim was found in the alley behind The Joker's Den, he told Frank what was known about the victim, that he was either a follower of the Bluegrass band the Lovey Doves, or he played in the band. He figured this much out from the tee shirt he was wearing.

Frank was shocked. His shock intensified the next day when he saw a close-up of the victim in the Sunday paper. The caption under the photo said, "If you recognize this young man, please contact Sheriff Houtman."

Frank phoned the sheriff immediately. "Sheriff, I-I-I'm calling about the picture of the murder victim in the paper this morning." Frank had a hard time holding himself together.

"Frank, do you know this kid?" asked Sheriff

Houtman.

"I think his name is Bobby, and he used to belong to a Bluegrass band called the Lovey Doves that I used to listen to in Chicago," sobbed Frank.

"You're the first person to come forward with any identification. We'll need to question you further to get any details of his life that you might know. Meet me at my office as soon as you can."

Frank had called Sam and asked him to come in early. "I have a personal emergency. I'll explain when you get here." When Sam arrived, Frank told him about the murder victim's picture in the paper and sobbed out that he was his son, Bobby.

Sam was livid. "We'll get to the bottom of this, Frank. Who would want to kill Bobby? Do you think Bobby was into drugs, buying them from Tyler at The Joker's Den?"

"Bobby would never do drugs. In one of her letters, Mary told me how upset he was when he discovered that several of the band members were using drugs. He threatened to turn them into the police and said he would find the person selling the drugs and beat him to a pulp. It took Mary a while to calm him down. The other night when Tyler was in, he was bragging about getting even with that kid that was trying to blackmail him. I think that kid was Bobby."

Chapter 56

Maybe Houtman Isn't So Clueless After All

After the Sheriff's interrogation, we were all exhausted and confused. I went to the bookstore and posted a Closed sign. We sat together in Sweet Indulgences and tried to eat dinner. Sadie had also posted a sign: Closed Until Further Notice. We couldn't face customers' questions and speculation, and the boys and Lola needed to be with us for support and comfort. Better to keep our shops closed and figure out what the next step should be. All of us were reeling from the news of Tyler's death. Our little town of Pittman, set against the mountains populated by families seeking refuge from the big cities has now seen two murders. Sadie and I tried to comfort the boys and Lola, but they were scared.

"Who could have done this, Mom?" asked Asher.

"Do you think there will be any more killings?" asked Billy.

"You don't think my dad could have done this, do you? I know he's been drinking again," said Mike.

"Do you think the sheriff will blame this on me? He still thinks I might have killed Bobby Jo and faked my kidnapping," said Billy.

"Don't worry, boys. We'll protect you. Sheriff Hoffman is smarter than you think he is. I'm sure he will get to the bottom of this," said Sadie.

"Let's just use our time to try to figure this out before the sheriff starts questioning us again. Lola, do you have a credible alibi if the sheriff questions you again?"

"I have an alibi. I was in Chicago like I said, but unless I can find the kid who spoke to me in the liquor store, the sheriff doesn't believe that I was there when Tyler was killed. He thinks I just faked the trip to give myself an alibi. I admit that I'm not sad Tyler is dead. I blame him for my parents' deaths, but I'm not a killer, an actress, yes, but not a killer."

"Billy, what is your alibi?" I asked.

"Well, Ms. George, I'm not sure. What time was Tyler killed? I was locked in a warehouse all weekend and wasn't rescued until Tuesday afternoon, though the sheriff doubts that I was kidnapped at all."

We kept at this line of inquiry trying to establish everyone's alibis. I put in a call to the sheriff's office to see if he wanted to join us for dinner, but Deputy Murphy said the sheriff would be tied up for awhile.

Chapter 57

The Sheriff Did It

As we all were going over the various alibis, Sheriff Houtman triumphantly burst into Sweet Indulgences followed by Deputy Murphy.

"Sheriff, we've been trying to reach you. Have you gotten any further in determining the murderer?" I asked.

He looked at us and said, "The cases are solved. First, Fergusson committed the robberies and vandalism to drive out the shop owners so he could build a multi-use development on Farley Square. Tyler assisted him, and Tyler even trashed his own store to throw suspicion off himself and to collect some needed insurance money. Tyler also is the one who wrote the slurs against Sadie. Sam and Frank clued us in on where to find the evidence since Tyler was bragging to them about executing Fergusson's plan to usurp all the property on Farley Square. Tyler also bragged about how much Fergusson was paying him to trash the shops."

Asher interrupted the sheriff, "See, I told you we didn't have anything to do with the crimes. I wish you had listened to us, Sheriff."

"I know. I know. I'm sorry, but I had to follow all leads, and you and Mike were seen casing The Joker's

Den."

"It was just innocent spying," Asher said.

"You see what innocent spying can lead to. From now on, you boys leave the snooping to the authorities, with a little assist from Sadie and me," I said with a grin.

The sheriff continued, "The state police arrested Fergusson as he was trying to board a flight at Hartford International Airport bound for Brazil. When the police brought him to us, he confessed to the burglaries, vandalism, and kidnapping. He was so arrogant. I don't think he has an ounce of remorse. He then proceeded to deny killing Tyler or Bobby Jo. He said that Tyler told him that Bobby Jo was blackmailing him, and he was going to take care of him."

"I knew Fergusson was crooked," Lola said. "Did you also investigate his side escort business? He provided paid escorts for any businesspeople who requested escort services. He tried to make me meet one of his clients at a hotel, but I was able to back out of it."

"I wasn't aware of that. I'll add it to the list of charges against him. We'll also see if he conducted that type of side business in Chicago before he was arrested and escaped.

"Also, we discovered that Tyler murdered Bobby Jo because Bobby Jo accused Tyler of selling the Lovey Dove band members the drugs that killed Lola's mother. Bobby Jo saw Lola's mom as a second mother who cared for him when she was sober. He intended to make Tyler quit providing drugs to the band, or Bobby Jo would turn him in to the sheriff for his crimes. Tyler knew then that he had to take drastic action to get rid of Bobby Jo. He arranged to meet Bobby Jo in the alley behind The Joker's Den. We found a partial print on the band trophy that killed Bobby Jo and were able to match it to Tyler. We also have Sam's testimony that at Ten Pins, he and Frank overheard Tyler bragging to Fergusson about getting rid of Bobby Jo."

"He killed my mom and dad with those drugs. If Tyler weren't already dead, I could kill him myself," sobbed over-dramatic Lola.

The sheriff continued, "The murder of Tyler is a bit more complicated. At first, we thought the murderer was Fergusson, but when the state troopers tracked him down, and we got a chance to question him, he denied trying to edge Tyler out of sharing in his profits, and he vehemently denied killing Tyler. Fergusson said he decided to escape town and leave Tyler in the dark as to where he fled. When we said that Fergusson's fingerprints were all over the counter in The Joker's Den, he gave in and told us that he was there at The Joker's Den, and had witnessed the murder. I asked him how he ended up at The Joker's Den just as the murder was being committed.

"Fergusson said, 'I intended to confront Tyler and scare him away from any further involvement in my real estate deals, and I was going to tell Tyler that our partnership was over, and I was leaving Pittman forever. I planned to tell Tyler he could do whatever he wanted, but he shouldn't contact me ever again. Before I could tell Tyler all this, I heard someone come in the door of The Joker's Den, so I hid behind the counter then I saw that person approach Tyler and vehemently bash him in the head while screaming, 'This is for the death of my son, you evil murderer.'"

"But who could that be?" Sadie asked. "I think

Fergusson is lying."

"Who is his father?" I asked.

"Was it Sam?" asked Mike. "Did my dad have another family that I didn't know about? Is that why he treated me so badly?"

"No, Mike," Sheriff Houtman said gently, "you are the only son that Sam has. Sam did admit to being involved in the kidnapping of Billy, but he said that Fergusson and Tyler threatened to kill or harm you if he didn't take part. I'm not sure if that was true or not. It's hard to get to the truth. We've determined that your dad was the guard that Murphy saw running from the warehouse. He'll probably do some time or be given probation considering the circumstances, but he's very contrite and really seems to want to do right by you."

"Okay, Sheriff, you've ruled everyone out. So, who killed Tyler? For the life of me, I can't figure it out," I confessed.

"Robin, Sadie, Lola, Asher, Mike, and Billy, though I appreciate your desire to help solve crimes, even by going to the extent of investigating me, you need to let the professionals handle the investigations."

Oops, I didn't realize the sheriff knew about our investigation into his wife's death. I wonder what else he knows about our snooping?

"We uncovered a motive for Tyler's murder when we interrogated Frank. Frank came into the office with his head down and tears in his eyes. He was shaking as he told us about Tyler's drunken bragging about killing Bobby Jo. Frank then handed me a picture of his wife Mary and their young son, Bobby. Then he handed me another picture of his grown son on stage in a band called the Lovey Doves' Bluegrass Band. When Frank saw the victim's picture in the paper, he knew then that the band member was his son Bobby.

"Frank sobbed, 'Tyler killed my only son. I swore I would never go to prison again, but I couldn't let that murderer get away with killing my boy.'

"We caught the murderer, but I hate that he is an avenging father," said the sheriff.

We were all silent at this news. We really wanted it to be sleazy Fergusson, not Frank who was trying so hard to turn his life around, but a father's anger is often too much to contain.

Sam said, "I feel bad for Frank. He's a good friend. I'll let him know I'll have a job for him after he serves his sentence since we hope the judge will go easy on a grieving father."

Sheriff Houtman said, "I will certainly put in a good word for Frank. A good lawyer might be able to get a verdict of temporary insanity because Frank was in shock over the murder of his son and wasn't responsible for his action."

Sam went back with the sheriff to talk to Frank and give him some support before he was taken away.

We all needed time to digest this news so I said, "Let's all go home now to give us time to think about all this. We'll see you back at Sadie's house tomorrow evening for dinner."

Chapter 58

Looking to the Future

Relief set in as we all processed the news the sheriff had given us and had a good night's sleep. We were ready to begin our normal lives again. Sadie closed Sweet Indulgences early, and at six-o-clock, a sumptuous dinner was laid out on the counter. Everyone began to tuck into shrimp, crabs, stuffed mushrooms, Kibbeh and pita bread, eggplant and sauce over rice, and chicken and hushweh. Sadie had outdone herself on the Lebanese food. I brought a beautiful cake decorated with Congratulations All on Your Super Sleuthing Skills. As we ate, we looked out the windows at the first major snowfall of the season. It was so beautiful and peaceful.

Sheriff Houtman arrived stomping the snow from his boots and presented Sadie with a beautiful poinsettia plant. Deputy Murphy came with a huge bouquet of yellow and white carnations for Lola. It seems he has been smitten with Lola since he first met her. Who would have guessed? Lola was blushing as she gratefully accepted his gift. You'd think Murphy had just presented her with an Academy Award.

Billy stood up and said, "I have something to confess. First, I want to thank everyone for searching for me and especially thank Sheriff Houtman and

Deputy Murphy for rescuing me. When I came to Pittman, Asher and Mike befriended me, and the band members took me in as one of their own, but I lied to everyone. I am so sorry. I almost told Sadie when I first stayed at her house, but I was afraid she would kick me out for lying."

"Billy," Sadie began, "I would never throw you out. Don't you know how much I care about you? You remind me of my brother Joseph, and it feels like you have given me a second chance at having a family."

Billy told the rest who hadn't heard about his parents dying, grandparents, and his Aunt Dehlia.

"I had to lie to you all because I was afraid someone would turn me into Children's Services. I'm sorry, everyone. I told all this to Ms. George and Sadie earlier, but I thought you all should know. I was desperate to stay here so I lied whenever personal questions were asked. Asher, needless to say, I don't need a wet head to do math. I took a shower each day in the locker room because I was living on the street."

"Don't worry, Billy," Sadie said. "We'll work this out somehow. I meant it when I said you are family, and families work out their problems. Robin and I talked, and with Sheriff Houtman's help, I'm willing to petition the court to adopt you, then you can continue to live with me. With the substantial money from your Aunt Dehlia's inheritance, the ongoing rights to all her books and movies, and the new *Fire, the Sleepy Dragon* book that we found in the safe deposit box at the bank, you should have an abundance of money to go on with your life quite comfortably in any career you should choose."

Mike jumped in, "Now that The Joker's Den is for

sale, Wayne plans to buy it if he can scrape together the money. He also hopes to eventually buy the Welcome Realty and make it a retail showroom for bikes and motorcycles. Maybe Billy can invest with him and become a partner in Wayne and Billy's Bike Repair Shop and a Motorcycle and Bike Sales Showroom."

"Great idea," we all said.

"I would love that. I'll call Wayne tomorrow to discuss a possible partnership."

Sadie looked at Sheriff Houtman with begging eyes.

"Okay, okay, Sadie. I'll look into the details, though Children's Services might have a problem with an unmarried woman who is an immigrant adopting an American orphan. We'll see what can be worked out."

Did Sheriff Mark Houtman just wink at Sadie when he said that? Look at him grinning. I can see that romance is in the air for Lola, Deputy Murphy, Sadie, and Mark Houtman.

I sat back quietly and closed my eyes, happy with my Farley Square family. I voiced a secret thought to my deceased husband, John.

Thank you for watching over all of us. Thank you for letting love bloom. Thank you for the great love you had for me and thank you for watching out for me and Asher. I will always love you.

Sadie's Favorite Lebanese Recipes

Kibbeh (kibbie)
Ingredients
2 ½ cups ground chuck
2 cups fine bulgur wheat
Season mixture of ground chuck and wheat with:
Salt- generous shake, then taste, and add more if needed
Pepper—about 2 heavy shakes
Garlic salt- about a teaspoon then taste and add more if needed
Ground cinnamon light
Stuffing
1 lb. ground lamb or ¾ cup minced lamb
Pine nuts about ½ cup
Brown these in butter and add salt, pepper, and cinnamon
Mix ground chuck and spices with the bulgur wheat.
Flatten ½ of the mixture into a 9 by 12 pan. Sprinkle the ground lamb and pine nuts evenly over the mixture. Cover with a second layer of ground chuck mixture. Leaving the rows intact, cut each row into diagonal rectangles. Into each row, place pats of butter evenly spaced.
Bake at 350 degrees for about ½ hour or until meat is brown.
The secret to success:
When you learn to cook Kibbeh, most experts say you should watch someone mix it, and taste it as they mix. Sadie's mom made her observe her grandmother cooking Kibbeh many times before she ever let Sadie

make it.

1 Ice is your friend. Soak bulgur wheat in 2 cups of iced water with ice in the measuring cup.

2 Keep ice on wheat as you mix with seasoned ground chuck. The colder your mixture, the more success you will have.

Because true Lebanese cooking is learned from observation, I have not given you exact measurements for spices. Tasting as you go along is your barometer.

Rice and Sauce and Eggplant

1 Rice–Cook according to package directions. Sadie usually used 1 cup of rice to 2 cups of water. Use long grain rice.

2 Sauce (Cook for several hours.)

½ can tomato paste

1 can tomato juice

1 can tomato sauce

1 small onion

Light salt, pepper, paprika, garlic salt, cinnamon

1 T sugar

Bring sauce to a boil, then cook on low heat for several hours.

3 While the sauce is cooking, brown 1 pound of ground lamb and ½ cup of pine nuts is 1 tablespoon of butter.

When brown, add to sauce and simmer.

4 1 eggplant

Peel and cut into slices diagonally. Put pieces on a microwavable dish covered with a paper towel and cover eggplant with another paper towel. Microwave for 5 minutes then place in a 9 by 12 baking dish.

When sauce has thickened, pour over eggplant, and cook at 350 for about 25 minutes. Sauce should be still moist, but not runny. Spoon sauce and eggplant over rice and serve.

Variation: Instead of eggplant, you can add a can of petite peas to the sauce mixture. No need for baking, just pour peas into sauce during the last ½ hour.

Hushweh

In 1T butter, brown ½ cup lamb bits from a chop or ground lamb and ½ cup of pine nuts. Add to rice while cooking.

Cook 1 cup long grain rice seasoned with light salt, pepper, and cinnamon in 2 cups of chicken broth until broth is absorbed.

Alternative: Instead of broth, use 2 cups water with 4 bouillon cubes.

Personal note from the author:

When my mother was engaged to my dad, she went to my grandmother's house for a week, for cooking lessons. My grandmother was known in the Lebanese community as one of the best cooks. She insisted that my mother could only learn to be a good cook if she watched and learned to measure spices not by teaspoons and tablespoons, but by tasting. When I learned to cook the Lebanese recipes as a young girl, I got a cookbook at the library and wanted to follow the recipes, but both my mother and my grandmother objected and insisted I learn the observe and taste method of seasoning. I like to think that I am now as good a cook as my mom.

One thing that differentiated my mom's cooking from my aunt's cooking was the use of Allspice. My aunt, who also was a good cook, used Allspice in her Kibbeh; my mom did not. Both are delicious.

A word about the author…

Ms. Jacobs is a writer, a teacher of Creative Writing, and a writing coach. She has published essays in various publications including Moida Quarterly Magazine, Kentucky Monthly Magazine, Motherwell online, KRTA News, and Teachers of Vision Magazine. She has published poems in various publications including Elephants Never online, SOS Art Cincinnati, and The Kentucky English Bulletin.

maryannjacobsauthor.wordpress.com

Thank you for purchasing
this publication of The Wild Rose Press, Inc.

For questions or more information
contact us at
info@thewildrosepress.com.

The Wild Rose Press, Inc.
www.thewildrosepress.com

Lightning Source UK Ltd.
Milton Keynes UK
UKHW020829060223
416538UK00016B/1851